WHEN YOU REMEMBER

Tawnya Torres

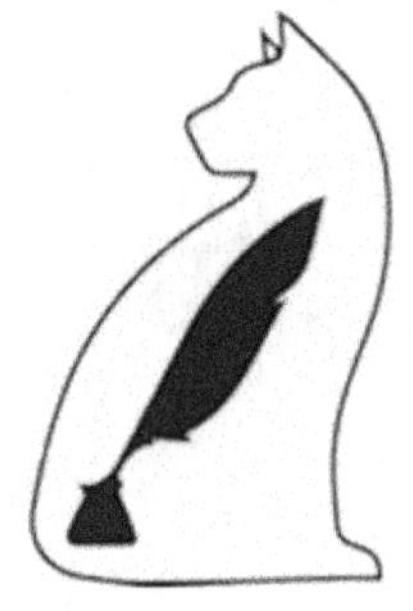

ISBN-13: 978-1-958557-55-6

Fireheart Press
1477 Hanford Ave.
Lincoln Park, MI 48146
editor@whitecatpublications.com

For Zac,

The person who taught me the most about love and without it, I would never be able to write what I write.

You are my hero, always.

PART ONE

Remember Me

CHAPTER ONE

Acquainted

Snowflakes drift down slowly and stick in her long, dark hair. She's spinning around causing the silk of her red kimono to lift and make sharp noises. Every step she takes melts the snow but leaves no soot. Aiya is always barefoot now. I offer her my cloak.

"Here, you're going to catch a cold," I say. She keeps dancing and flipping her hair over her shoulder.

"I'm never cold," she says in her low and husky voice.

I put it on her anyway and she smiles. Her canines are sharper than mine but they do not diminish her beauty. She is perfect. We walk hand in hand through the white and gray in a peaceful silence. I'm still not sure what to say to her most of the time but we are happy to have centuries to get acquainted. Without reason Aiya stops and kisses me. She has been very affectionate towards me since her transformation. Before I can open my eyes she's gone.

"Aiya?" I don't see her anywhere.

Looking in every direction I search for dissolved snow but the ground is powdery and without footprints.

"Aiya? Where are you?" There is a pounding in my chest and I feel the frosty air freeze the breath in my lungs.

"Aiya!" I call her name a third time and she jumps on me from one of the cedars and knocks me into the snow. "Hey! What are you doing?" I ask.

She covers her rosy mouth with her hands and giggles. I want to be upset with her but I'm not. She's having fun and I don't want to spoil her good mood.

"I'm sorry, Riku. I was just playing," she says and my heart melts.

"It's okay." I brush the snow off my shoulder. She scoots closer and shakes the snow from my hair and smiles at me again.

"I love you," she says.

"I love you." I help her to her feet even though she doesn't need my assistance. Aiya is strong and capable of taking care of herself but she doesn't seem bothered by my overprotectiveness.

"Riku, can I ask you something?"

"Of course. You can ask me anything."

"What's your favorite color?" Her question surprises me with its simplicity.

"What's your favorite color?" I ask. She stops walking and I look over to see her bright red eyes staring up at me.

"That's not how this works. You always say you like whatever I like. But I want to know you," she says in a serious tone. I didn't realize my preferences would matter to her.

"Green, like the pines." This answer pleases her and we resume walking.

"My favorite color is red," she says as she looks at the ground.

I think red reminds her of Kasai but she tries her best not to let him take anything away from her. We pass a large deer, a buck. He stands as a majestic beast and watches us as we glide by.

"What's your favorite flower?" she asks.

I haven't thought much about flowers or favorites. When I lived in the northern mountains I enjoyed the hills turning blue in the spring with thousands of blossoms.

"Baby blue eyes," I say. She gives me a thoughtful nod as she breaks from my grasp and starts spinning around again.

"Red spider lilies," she says and her hair fans out around her.

I already knew this. Since I've met her she's had these red spider lily hair sticks. I assume they are sentimental. She takes my hand and begs me to dance with her. The snowflakes land on her eyelashes. They reach her eyebrows. They melt as they touch her cheek.

"What's your favorite food?"

"Salmon. What about you?" She gives me a sly grin.

"I love spicy mussels." I make a face at her. I hate spicy food. She laughs and I find myself laughing as well.

"Hey guys!" It's Hanako.

Her red and black ears stand out against the white and gray. Aiya runs to embrace our fox friend. Hanako picks her up and swings her around. I see she has a bundle on her back.

"Hello, Hanako. What's going on?" I ask.

"I received a message. My father would like to see me. I'm going back home for the winter. I haven't seen him in three years. I miss him," she says.

"Is something wrong?" Aiya asks with concern.

"No, everything is fine. It's just time for me to return to the western demon fox tribe." Aiya holds onto Hanako and strokes her starlight hair.

"I'll miss you," she whispers.

"Don't worry, I'll never abandon you. Winter won't be forever. Where do you guys want me to meet you in the spring?" asks Hanako. She runs her delicate fingers through Aiya's ink black hair. She always knows what to say.

"Meet us at my village."

"Okay! I'll see you two when the cherry blossoms start to bloom. Take care," says Hanako. She hugs Aiya and then me. She holds me a moment longer and whispers in my ear, "I know you'll take good care of her."

Hanako is the first friend I've ever had. I grew up in a strict household as a soldier with no purpose other than war and wealth. Besides my siblings and Hoshi, I didn't socialize. The fox girl's kindness is immeasurable.

"Goodbye, Aiya! Bye, Riku!"

"Goodbye, Hanako! Don't forget me," says Aiya. The fox girl stops and looks over her shoulder at us.

"I could never forget you," she says. Hanako disappears into the white abyss. I realize this is the first time Aiya and I have truly been alone since we left her village. This makes me nervous.

"Where do you want to go?" I ask her. She puts her hand to her chin and ponders my question.

"I've been having so much fun here with you. But I kind of miss my home as well. Would you mind if we spent the winter there? I haven't visited Chiyo..." She holds her arm and looks at the ground. Aiya thinks I'm going to say "no" but I would never deny her of anything.

"I will go anywhere you want to go."

***

We travel to Aiya's village hand in hand. If she's not touching me she's dancing and melting the snow. I think about the first time we spoke and how she thought I didn't remember her. There's so much about me Aiya doesn't know but I'm not sure where or how to begin. I still don't know how she learned my name.

I'm grateful she loves me anyway. She is unaware of her affect on me. When she sings my heart aches. We lay on the ground cheek to cheek and she rests her left hand on my temple as we watch the snow come down from the heavens.

"Riku, can I ask you something?"

"Yes," I say.

"What's your favorite season?"

"Winter."

I turn and kiss her. The stars on her face stand out against her pale skin and the white abyss. "What's your favorite season?"

"My baby brother was born during the winter solstice. I have loved this time of year ever since," she says and I can see the reflection of snowflakes in her scarlet eyes.

"What was your sister's name?" I ask. I feel like I shouldn't but I can't help myself.

"Her name was Emi. She was a year younger than me," she says. Aiya answers me without any hint of annoyance.

"I'm sorry about your family, Aiya."

This is the second time I've mentioned anything about them. She sits up and snow falls from her shoulders and long hair. Her eyes look at me with an expression I can't read.

"What about your family, Riku?" Her voice is sad but curious.

"What about them?"

"Do you ever miss them?" I think about her question for a few moments before I answer.

"I miss my sisters Yama and Yuri." A snowflake lands in my eye, blurring my vision.

"Why don't you ever visit them?" she asks.

"Yama still lives in the northern mountains. I am banished from there. My baby sister Yuri is like me. She went to live in a village with a human boy." As the words leave my mouth I see Aiya shed a tear. "Don't cry for me. It's okay."

"I'm sorry."

"Don't be. I'm not." I pull her to my chest.

"Can I ask you another question?"

"You can ask me as many questions as you want."

"Where is your favorite place?"

"Wherever you are," I say.

This seems to make Aiya feel better and we continue walking. Our bodies leave imprints in the snow. As we walk she picks the sunny daffodils and begins making a necklace with them. At first I think she's going to place it on herself but she puts it on me instead. Aiya's small but sweet gestures make my face feel hot against the frozen air.

"My mother and I used to sit in the meadow where the red spider lilies grew. When the wind blew it looked like scarlet waves. A red ocean," says Aiya.

I have wondered about her mother. Aiya said she was more beautiful than her. The birds would wait for her to sing to them. I wish I could have had the pleasure of meeting her.

Aiya's father is a thorn in my thoughts though. How he could do something so cruel to someone he loved disgusts me. I try not to show my disdain. I know she still misses him. The night I met Aiya I walked through a field of red spider lilies to get to her village. I know the place she is talking about.

"Riku, look!" she says excitedly.

She pulls me towards a rocky hot spring surrounded by peonies and cedar trees. Aiya begins gathering small blossoms, stems, and leaves. She takes her armful of treasures and places them on one of the boulders. Uninhibited, she takes off her kimono. I'm still reserved around Aiya and feel awkward about her lack of modesty around me.

She disappears into the steamy water for a moment and when she surfaces she throws back her long hair. The swiftness of it reminds me of the water dragon.

"Are you going to join me?" she asks. As I get into the hot spring with her she uses a small rock to grind the flower petals and stems into a paste.

"What are you doing?" I ask. She takes a handful of the floral product and puts it in my hair. It smells herbal and sweet.

"Lady Kiyori taught me about the properties in certain plants. This will make your hair soft and smell good."

She uses the rest in her inky locks that now hug her body. I glance at her out of the corner of my eye but try not to directly look at her. She starts laughing which tempts me to stare up at her.

"What's so funny?"

"Nothing," she giggles.

"Please. Tell me." I'm beginning to feel anxious.

"It's just that I didn't expect you to be so..." she covers her mouth to conceal her smile.

"So what?" I ask.

"So pure."

"Is that a bad thing?"

"No, of course not."

She disappears under the water and I watch the steam rise from the clear liquid. The falling snow is refreshing against my feverish face. Aiya hasn't come up yet and I'm getting worried.

"Aiya?" I wade into the middle of the hot spring. She is always doing this to me now. I know she is just playing but it makes me cross.

"Come on, Aiya." I look into the water and see nothing but rocks. "This isn't funny anymore!"

I can't contain my irritation. There are slender arms around me and she squirts water in my face through her pouty lips. I almost yell at her but she is happy and I can't take that away from her.

"I'm sorry, Riku." The change in her tone erases my anger immediately.

"It's okay." I put my arms around her and she rests her head against my chest. She looks up at me and grabs my shoulders to pull me under the water where she kisses me for a long time. I would drown if this was the only way. My gasping for air entertains her and she continues to laugh as she wrings out the water from her hair. The texture of our skin changes and we get out of the hot spring.

"I'll be there in a minute. Go ahead without me." She looks at me confused but Aiya tends to do what I say.

"Okay," she says and waves at me. Once she's far enough away I call out the cat.

"Come out," I growl.

"Are you talking to me?" The tiger demon hangs on a branch from his legs.

"Do you always make a habit out of watching people during their private moments?"

"Only when it's you or that little mouse of yours," he laughs with his wildcat trill. I jump into the tree and land on the branch he's on. This makes his eyes widen.

"Don't you remember what I said?"

"You said don't talk to her. You never said anything about looking at her."

He flashes me his smug grin. The blood turns black in my veins and I chase after him through the canopy. To my surprise the tiger demon is extremely agile and eludes me with ease. I lose track of him in the treetops. I don't want to keep Aiya waiting so I hop down and make my way towards her.

The next time I see the tiger demon I'm going to sink my jaws into his throat. How dare he show such disrespect! I hated seeing him eye her down with his predatory gaze clothed but knowing he saw her naked body begs me to be consumed by demonic hatred. I try to let go of my anger as I walk up beside Aiya.

"What were you doing?" she asks.

"Nothing, I just thought I saw something."

***

The sun is out, casting an ethereal glow on the frozen ground. Aiya is putting peonies and daffodils in her hair. She reaches up and I lean down so she can put one behind my ear as well. I kiss her and she holds my face for a moment. There are times I think she isn't going to let go but I wouldn't mind.

"Riku, can we talk about something?" she asks.

"Of course. What is it?"

"I want to know you. I want to know everything about you. I hate to ask but I need to understand. Why are you banished from the northern mountains? What happened with your father and siblings?" Her hair falls in her face and I brush it out of her eyes. I am honest with her.

"My disloyalty, my disobedience, it cost me my status and my place in our family. The day of the challenge I fled. I was disgraced after that," I say.

"You said your older brother took the crown. What is he like?" Aiya stares ahead and plays with her hair, braiding and unbraiding it. I can tell she is nervous but I'm not angry about her curiosity.

"My older brother Ryo is an arrogant imbecile. Cold and merciless. He cut our father's head off to be king. Then he tempted me to murder him so I would be forced into leading. Our culture demands us to be selfless and worship the alpha as divine." Aiya squeezes my hand and looks up at me with tears in her lash line. I feel guilty for making her sad, "I'm sorry, Aiya. Please, don't cry."

"Are you okay, Riku?" Her question shocks me.

"I'm fine. Don't worry about me," I say and kneel down to wipe away her tears.

She wraps her arms around my neck and holds me with such intensity it leaves me unable to speak. Aiya is crying and it's all my fault. Hot, salty tears pool down her cheeks. They run down her neck until they reach my lips.

"You always say you're okay," she whispers. I pull away to look her in the eyes.

"I am. Really, I am."

"You can tell me if you aren't. You can tell me anything. I'm here for you." Her husky voice is shaky.

"I would never lie to you. I promise," I say.

"You promise?"

"I promise."

This cheers her up and she goes back to dancing, causing the flowers in her hair to fall out and land in the snow. I'm happy Aiya doesn't stay sad for very long anymore. I try not to live in the past but there are rocks in my stomach when I think about her sad pouty face and the tears she cried while she sang about me.

"Riku?" She brings me out of my thoughts.

"Yes?"

"I need to know something."

"What is it?" She looks at the ground and refuses to meet my gaze.

"Why didn't you come back for me?" she asks. Aiya is holding her left wrist and clenching her fist. I think of Kasai's ability to invade her dreams and I wonder if she can read my mind.

"I did once. But I was too afraid to approach you. I'm sorry," I admit. Aiya's expression is a mix of relief and hurt. I pick her up by her waist and she holds my shoulders as I spin her around which makes her smile again. "Three summers after we met I heard you singing about me. I have loved you ever since. I never stopped thinking about you."

"Why were you afraid to approach me?" she asks.

"I'm not sure. I think I was afraid you wouldn't love me back," I confess. Aiya has a sly grin on her face as we walk. She giggles for a moment.

"Hajime knew I loved you before I knew it myself. On my sixteenth birthday he told me how he felt about me. I rejected him though. He never brought it up again but occasionally I'd see him watching me stare into the forest. I didn't know what I was doing at the time but he knew I was waiting for you."

Aiya's confession is bittersweet. I'm lucky to have someone so perfect to love me. Yet I am vexed–Aiya has someone better than I who loves her. I know she did not tell me this to annoy me. I hide my irritation. Hajime saved her life and I will be forever grateful to him.

"Do you regret not marrying Hajime?" I ask. The question leaves my mouth without much thought. I brace myself.

"No. Hajime is a good friend. He has always let me be myself even if that meant I didn't include him in my life." Her admission hits me in the heart with a pang of anger. I don't know why I'm upset but I am. She continues, "Have you ever been married?" My frustration turns to shame as she cringes waiting for my reply.

"No, but I was engaged. It was an arranged marriage."

"What was her name?"

"Hoshi." I haven't said her name in over a decade. It leaves a tart aftertaste on my tongue.

"Was she pretty?" Aiya isn't jealous but her body is tense with insecurity. She continues to massage the skin on her wrist with worry.

"Not as pretty as you," I say.

"Really?"

"Yes, really."

"Did you love her?"

"I cared about her but I didn't love her. I've never loved anyone the way I love you." Aiya studies my face to make sure I'm being genuine. She runs her dainty hands through my hair and looks into my eyes.

"What happened to her?" she asks.

"She married my older brother," I say in a flat tone. Aiya opens her mouth like she wants to say something but she can't get the words out. "It's okay, really. I'm not upset about it."

"I'm sorry, Riku. I had no idea what you've been through. I shouldn't ask you so many questions." She hangs her head but I reach under her chin and force her to face me.

"Don't be sorry. You never have to be sorry."

CHAPTER TWO

Homecoming

Aiya skips in front of me as we near her village. I look over my shoulder to the left and stare at the hill where Kasai changed her. She doesn't even glance at it. The village is quiet. The snow muffles the voices and the bird songs. We are greeted by Natsume, Hiromi, and Daina.

"Aiya! Riku! You're back," exclaims Hiromi.

"We've missed you," says Natsume.

"We've all missed you!" adds Daina. Aiya takes Hiromi's hands and smiles at all three of them.

"We've missed you, too."

Aiya speaks for both of us. It's not that I don't like the people of Aiya's village but I am at a loss for words. I put my arm around her and nod my head to let them know I'm paying attention. They all stare at me and their faces turn hot pink. I wonder what I did.

"You must be exhausted. Go home and get some rest," chimes Natsume.

She hugs Aiya and so does Daina. We both wave goodbye. I notice Hiromi and Daina look like they're going to faint. Aiya takes my hand in hers as we walk through the village. Not too many people are out. It's probably too cold for them. I love the frigid weather. Something about it makes me feel alive.

Through the snowy veil we see bright scarlet. Three priestesses walk past us in their red trousers. Their long hair moves with the wind and the paper ribbon makes crinkling noises in the breeze. Two of them carry swords and the tallest girl has a bow and arrows.

One of the young women has juniper eyes and light hair. She reminds me of Hoshi. I feel bile build in my throat and I swallow. We get to Aiya's house and she starts the fire with her hand. It takes no effort. I remove my armor and cloak. She straightens the collar of my shirt and rubs my shoulders.

"I'll be right back. Wait here," she says and moves out the door like a ghost.

I've never been in Aiya's home before. She invited me in when we first came back in the summer. I felt it was improper at the time. My eyes drift around the room and I study her belongings. I know I shouldn't but I get up and run my hand over her different colored kimonos. Shades of blue, red, and yellow. I pick up the buttercup one. It reminds me of the day I heard her sing about me. I hope she doesn't get mad if she catches me pawing through her things. I can't stop myself.

She has a white and red teapot with four matching cups. There's a small table in the corner with a large white bowl and a mirror. She has a comb that looks like it's made from some kind of bone. There are two containers with powder in them. The first one smells like roses and the other is a mix of lily and nightflower. Upon further inspection I find a clear vial with an amber oil in it. This one smells like oranges and cherry blossoms.

The only item I haven't explored is her bed. I feel shy about this. It's a simple mat with white blankets and white pillows. I haven't slept in one since I left home. Ignoring my shyness I decide to make myself comfortable. It's soft and even though she hasn't been here in several months it still smells like her. Everything in her house is coated in the honey and tea leaf fragrance. Aiya's back with a tray.

"I told Hiromi your favorite food is salmon and she made you these." She offers me a rice ball. It has salmon and seaweed in it. It's salty but it's good.

"Thank you. She didn't have to do that," I say.

"She said she wanted to," says Aiya. I'm frustrated. I think it's because I assumed I would be taking care of Aiya but more often than not she is the one taking care of me.

"Are you happy to be home?" I ask.

"I'm always happy now."

***

It feels like I've slept for only a moment but I wake up to a knock on the door. It's the monk. He looks at me and then down at Aiya and his face turns red.

"What is it, Brother Minoru?" I ask.

"Something is coming this way." He barely finishes his sentence and I'm awake. I throw on my armor and grab my sword.

"Which way is it coming from?"

"It's coming from the east. I sensed a dark presence in the night. I thought it would pass but it is headed straight for us," he says.

Lady Kiyori and the priestesses are waiting. I follow the monk who is swift on his feet. He flies like a crane, graceful and calm. I see red in the white abyss. There are seven priestesses in a line facing the east with their weapons drawn. Lady Kiyori approaches us.

"Riku, thank you for joining us," she says.

"Do you know what's headed here?" I ask.

"No. Brother Minoru can't tell what it is, only that it has an evil aura like the centipede."

Her lips are tight and her jaw is clenched. Brother Minoru and I follow her to join the priestesses. They stare at me as I near them. I get in front and listen for it. At first there is nothing but then it hits me. The undeniable squealing of a filthy pig.

"It's the boar demons," I announce. The priestesses look at one another and then at Lady Kiyori.

"What should we do?" asks Brother Minoru.

"Stay here," I say and go back to listening for the boar demons. The hooves tear up the land and destroy the ground. As they draw closer I can hear the rumble in the distance. It's a small group, not an army. Nothing like the last war I fought with my father. I take off in the direction of the horrible sound. Lady Kiyori keeps calling my name but I don't turn around. I can't let them get hurt.

The further I am from the village the better. Snow falls from the pines and the ground vibrates from the stampede coming right at me. I see them. There are two dozen of them. Not as many as I thought.

I draw my blade and begin cutting them down. One by one I slice through them. Decapitating or hacking off their limbs, I do what I have to. It's my duty to protect Aiya and the people she loves. I lock my sword with the tusks of a larger boar demon and see the glazed over eyes. They are crusted with infection and he smells of rot. I put my weapon through his chin and up into his brain. The demonic aura emanates black mist from their chipped hooves.

They squeal and spittle flies everywhere. Filthy pigs. Their vile black blood mixes with the scent of their decaying flesh and it stings my eyes. I throw my blade through three of them and the snow turns into black slush beneath them. Picking up my weapon I feel the air shift. Looking over my shoulder I see the tusks and then I hear the scream. He hits me in the right shoulder and knocks my sword out of my hand. He stomps on me but I shove my left hand into his chest and rip out his heart. The wound oozes purple and black tar before the body begins disintegrating.

I pick up a handful of snow and wipe the toxic blood off my arm. There are a few blisters but no serious injury. Two of the disgusting beasts are running in the direction of the village and I give chase. They are fast but dull. Coming up behind them I jump and drive my blade through the bigger boar's head. He falls in a heap and the putrid scent of his guts permeates the chilly air. The other one is approaching Aiya's village and I make my way to slice him in half. The eyes bulge and fall out, rolling down the hill. The ruby eyes stand out against the paper white snow. The pig's intestines write out his story in black ink.

There are four stragglers left and I hunt them down one by one. Their diminished intelligence has led them away from the village but they are still a threat. Boars pollute the land with their demonic aura. The darkness has rotted them to the core. One of the boar demons grazes me with his dirty tusks but I drive my blade into his mouth. It drips with saliva reeking of spoiled meat. Their teeth are broken and make their home in decomposing gums. The blood in their bodies is poisonous even to themselves. Everything about them is repulsive.

I jump and land in front of another one and hack his head off. Blood sprays my face and it sizzles where it touches me. I let out a hoarse scream. The pain blinds me momentarily. I shake away the frayed edges and go after the last of the boar demons. The squeal rings in my ears but I am ready for it. I turn to my right and drive the sword in between its eyes. The stomach of this one is bumpy and the teats drip foamy brown milk. This one is a sow. With the last one in front of me I aim carefully and throw my blade into its chest. Sour green liquid seeps out of the snout and he falls over dead with a hole through his body.

Scanning around I see that I have taken down the group by myself. I am thankful to have arrived here in time. I couldn't stand Aiya losing anyone else she loves. I head back towards the monk and the priestesses.

"Riku, are you okay?" asks the monk.

"I'm fine."

"What about your shoulder?" asks Lady Kiyori.

She points to the gash in my arm. Blood seeps out and proves her point as it paints the snow with red ink.

"I can handle it," I say. My answer doesn't satisfy her and she takes my hand in hers. The priestess has creamy skin and long fingers. She gingerly examines the blisters on my hand and the injury to my shoulder.

"Please, let me help you," she says.

I don't want to be rude so I nod to agree. I look down as we walk to the temple and I notice there's blood all down my right side and splashed across my armor. None of the priestesses seem frightened of me but they keep glancing in my direction.

Once we are at the temple Lady Kiyori has me sit down. She removes my armor and I see her admire the prestigious steel. It must be interesting to her because she keeps looking at it as she cleans my wound.

"What does that symbol mean?" she asks.

"It's the northern demon wolf insignia."

"Your armor, it's heavy. Very expensive."

"Yes. Our people are excessively wealthy. Our weapons, our food, our clothes are lavish and ridiculous," I say, a bit too harsh. The priestess stops to look at me. I think this is the first time she's really seen me.

"Why did you leave your home?"

Her face is stony but pretty. She has elegant features. A tiny nose, thick eyelashes, prominent round cheeks, and kind brown eyes.

"Demon wolf culture demands us to fight the alpha. I refused and was disgraced for it," I say.

My reply causes the priestess to grin ever so slightly. She has finished bandaging my shoulder and is now tending to my hand. Lady Kiyori has a quiet way of showing she cares. The ointment she puts on my blisters smells like pine needles and camphor. I'm glad Aiya had someone to teach her about remedies and antidotes. It makes me feel better knowing she had a woman like the priestess to raise her. I'm lost in my thoughts but Lady Kiyori's hand on my chest surprises me.

"You have a good heart. I don't think you would kill anybody if you didn't have to. Thank you for helping us today. I know it must weigh heavy on your soul. We are forever indebted to you. Please, let me know if you need anything. If you ever want to talk, me and Brother Minoru are always willing to listen," she says. Lady Kiyori goes back to wrapping my hand.

"Thank you."

I wish I could say more but I'm speechless. I wave goodbye to the priestess and she gives me a thoughtful bow. The sun is setting. The nights are long this time of year. The sky is blue-dark by the time I get to Aiya's house.

"Riku! I was worried about you. Where did you go?" she asks.

"Lady Kiyori and Brother Minoru needed my help." Aiya looks me up and down and notices the blood on my armor and the bandages. She pulls me inside and has me sit with her.

"What happened?"

"There was a small army of boar demons. I was able to kill them by myself. I didn't want anybody to get hurt," I say. Aiya is careful not to touch my injuries but she puts her arms around me.

"Are you okay?" she asks with shiny crimson eyes.

"I'm fine, Aiya. I promise."

"Thank you for protecting my family."

"I would do anything for you."

Aiya looks at my shoulder and my hand. I think she wants to say something but instead she kisses me for a long time. I think she feels protective of me and I smile at the thought.

***

I wake up with my shoulder throbbing and a profuse sting in my hand. Aiya isn't sleeping next to me. I reach for my clothes but they're gone. The pain in my shoulder travels down my spine and I give in. Laying down is uncomfortable. My body hasn't hurt like this in years.

Turning to my side I reach for where Aiya should be. I wonder where she went. Normally I would be agitated about this but the fierce ache in my right side leaves me with little energy. I am too tired to be annoyed. Breathing in the fragrant honey and tea leaf smell I feel myself relax.

"Riku?" Aiya is back.

"Hey," I rasp.

I try to sit up but I wince in pain and grab my shoulder. Pulling my hand away I see blood. The wound is reopening and red ink escapes the bandage.

"Don't move so fast."

Her eyes are sad as she kneels down next to me. She's brought a basket with her. With petite hands she fishes out more bandages and a round container. Thin fingers remove the soaked bandages. Pouring hot water into the large white bowl by the mirror she mixes in a powder. It smells minty and sterile. My blood stains many white towels crimson as she cleans the deep gash from the boar demon's tusks. She wraps my shoulder and I grit my teeth as she ties the bandage.

"Thank you," I say.

"You don't have to thank me."

Now she's examining my palm. She dips a new towel in the herbal water and squeezes it into my hand. I almost scold her. It hurts so bad but I can't raise my voice to her. She caresses my palm and the stinging subsides. When she pulls the towel away there are splotches of dark red. The toxic blood is slowing my healing. She wraps my hand and secures it at my wrist where there are berry sized burns. The effervescent water has taken the sting out of my palm.

"It feels much better."

Aiya looks at me with that unreadable expression. I can't analyze her face anymore because she is going through the basket again.

"I brought you breakfast and washed your clothes," she says. Aiya puts down my bodysuit and undershirt. She places an apple and a bowl of steamy lotus roots next to me.

"Thanks," I say.

I'm sincere but the intense soreness in my body has made me lose my appetite and I want to disappear inside myself. Aiya must sense I want to be left alone.

"I'm going out for a little bit. I'll check on you soon, okay?" She gives me a soft kiss but is gone before I can open my eyes. I feel guilty about my behavior. Why have I been so tense lately?

I'm not hungry but I eat anyway. It will increase the speed of my healing. She left me a container of water as well and I drink it all. I need my body to be fully functional. It's unintentional but I fall asleep until it's dark out. I look for Aiya but she's not here. The fire is lit though. She must have been here earlier. Sitting up is easier but still sends a shooting pain up and down my spine. I lay down and embrace defeat.

"Hey, Riku. How are you feeling?" It's Chiyo. Aiya and Haru are in the doorway.

"Hi, Chiyo. I'm okay."

The girls sit across from me and Aiya sits next to me. She rests her hand on the back of my neck. Looking past the fire I study Yuta's wife. I've never seen anyone with hair like hers. She has wavy brown hair but it has streaks of blonde and copper in it. I don't want to make her uncomfortable. I resort to staring into the fire.

"Thank you for protecting us, Riku," says the young woman with auburn and sunshine hair.

"You're welcome." I wish to say more but my lungs are tired and sore from pushing against my bruised rib cage.

"Do you need anything?" asks Aiya. Her hand is a fever against my skin but it's soothing.

"No, I'm fine."

I close my eyes and listen to the girls talk for a few moments. I feel someone staring at me. I open one eye and catch Haru watching me. Her eyes are chestnut like Hanako's. I ignore it and pretend I don't see her.

"I'm really happy to see you two. You seem very in love. It's so sweet," says Chiyo.

I look up to see her with her hands clasped. Dark blue eyes sparkle like the ocean. She is a bright and cheery person. It's hard to be glum around her.

"It's good to be home," says Aiya.

I let her speak for both of us. The sound of silk dragging on wood and a shuffle across the floor forces me to open my eyes. Haru is kneeling down next to me.

"Can I touch your hair?" she asks.

I turn to Aiya and she nods to give her permission. Haru is a few years younger than Chiyo and Aiya. Probably the same age Aiya was when I first heard her sing about me. Yuta's wife has silky hands that are tiny, smaller than Aiya's. She uses her petite fingers to lift the bangs covering my eyes.

"Wow," the word escapes her cherry mouth. She has a dimple on her left cheek and her top lip is fuller than her bottom lip, giving her a youthful appearance.

"What?" I ask.

"You are flawless. I've never seen someone as gorgeous as you." The young girl's answer startles me and I feel myself becoming shy. Chiyo covers her mouth but I can still hear her muffled giggle.

"Thank you," I mumble. I'm not sure what to say. Humans, especially women, often confuse me. I want to be her friend though because she is Aiya's friend, "Your hair is very beautiful. I've never seen anything like it." My compliment causes her face to flush.

"Really?" she asks.

"Yes, I swear." She touches her copper laced bark and sunshine tresses.

"Thank you," she says as she gazes dreamily into the flames. She is smiling to herself.

"Oh, before I forget!" says Chiyo.

She darts out the door but returns a moment later with two large bowls. She offers them to me and Aiya. "I made you two dinner. It's rice porridge with salmon." She smiles at me. Aiya must have told her.

"You didn't have to do that, Chiyo. Thank you," I say.

"I wanted to. It brings me joy to cook for the people I love. You two need your rest. Enjoy your dinner. I'll see you tomorrow! Goodnight."

Chiyo waves at us and Haru follows. She peeks over her shoulder to get one last look at me. Aiya helps me sit up and I take a few bites. Everything still hurts. I don't want to come off as unappreciative so I finish my food and lie down.

"I missed you today. Did you miss me?" asks Aiya. She pulls back the blanket and examines my arm. Deciding she doesn't need to change the bandage she gets into bed with me. I put the uninjured hand on her hip and stroke the dip down her side. It hurts my shoulder but I do it anyway.

"I always miss you," I say.

"I never want to be without you."

"You won't be. I'm right here."

CHAPTER THREE

Armed with Stars and Flames

The sun rises and I open my eyes to find Aiya's arm around me, her palm resting on my heart. She has freckles on her elbows, collar bone, and navel. They are shades of tan, copper, and umber. I have tried to keep these things a mystery to me but she is uninhibited in my presence. As gently as I can I untangle myself from her grasp without waking her. I get dressed and wash my face. Her mouth is rosy and slightly parted. I kiss her goodbye and slip out the door.

I love Aiya more than anything but there are times when I have to be by myself. Beyond the cedars, camphors, and hydrangeas, I slink into the depths of the forest. There's a flying squirrel following me. We make eye contact but it shows no fear and keeps hopping from branch to branch above me.

My shoulder is almost done healing. There is a hint of purple and yellow to it but it has stopped bleeding. The wound is closed. I take the bandage off my hand and find the blisters are gone. The burns have disappeared as well. There is a red thread on the right shoulder of my bodysuit. Aiya must have sewed it for me. I put my palm to it and my heart is warm in my chest thinking about her fixing my clothes and taking care of me when I'm hurt.

There's a stream up ahead and I use the fresh water to clean my hands. I run it through my hair and shake clear droplets everywhere. It feels good to be by myself. I never leave Aiya for long but I do sneak away on occasion. She lets me have my space but I know she wonders where I go and worries that I won't come back. I'll be with Aiya forever, I couldn't bear us being apart, but I need to be alone sometimes.

"Hey there, pretty boy." The familiar voice is in the trees to the left and I manage to land on the branch where the tiger demon is.

"What do you want?"

"I was wondering why you're all by yourself. Did your little mouse leave you?" he asks.

"No. She wouldn't do that," I growl at him. He throws his head back with a smug smirk.

"I know. I can tell." He examines his claws and makes no move to run from me.

"What do you mean?" I'm sure he is going to trick me but I am curious what he has to say.

"That girl is so in love with you it's actually kind of disgusting. And you're one sick puppy, my friend!" His vocal cords vibrate with his roaring laughter.

"I'll take that as a compliment," I mutter.

"You should. I've never seen two people in love the way you and that little mouse are. See ya around, pretty boy," he says.

The tip of the orange tail vanishes in the treetops. I make an effort to see where he went but he has the upper hand. I am in his territory. Everywhere the scent of a cat cloys the air. I came out here to relax but now I am cross.

The tiger demon confuses me. Was he being genuine or mocking me? I can't tell. He didn't seem jealous. More of an abstract observer. The wildcat's voyeurism vexes me. There's a large lake ahead. It's not frozen beyond the dark woods. Not caring if the tiger is watching me or not I take off my clothes and wade into the chilly water and hold my breath. Coming up for air I feel refreshed and less anxious.

Swimming for a while I stare up at the gray sky. Birds call to one another and fly over me. I stare at their shadows as they dart across the snow. Aiya is probably worried about me. I should get back to her. Shaking the water from my hair I feel the wolf within. I have broken myself of most habits but there are skeletons in my personality.

Walking back to Aiya's village I find an array of winter flowers. I pick three white roses, a couple pink peonies, and half a dozen daffodils for her. I'm disappointed to find she's not home. I put her bouquet in the water canteen. It's early evening but I'm tired. I sit outside and watch the sunset. The creamy orange sky makes the snow sparkle gold and silver. I wish Aiya was here to watch this with me.

I take off the armor and peel out of my bodysuit. Crawling into bed I am hit with her decadent honey scent. I lay on Aiya's side and rest my head on her pillow. How is it possible to love someone so much it's almost unbearable? I ponder this thought as I fall asleep.

At first I think it's a dream but it's not. The fire is lit and Aiya has her arms and legs wrapped around me. The flames turn her hair into shiny red and black ink. The blanket is at my knees and I reach down for it to see her exposed thigh hugging my waist. I decide to rest my hand there and close my eyes.

She nudges my chin with her nose and undoes the collar of my shirt so she can kiss my neck. It's nice at first but it's distracting and I can't sleep anymore. She's breathing into my ear and I feel myself start to lose control.

"Please don't," I say.

"Do you not like when I kiss you?"

"I like it too much." I smile at her.

Her lips are pouty but she turns up the corners of her mouth as I play with her hair. I pull the long black curtain to the nape of her beautiful neck and I fold it over my wrist so I can hold more of her.

"We don't have to wait."

"I want to wait." I let her inky locks fall from my palm before I pick them back up again.

"Why?" she asks.

"I just do. Please, it's important to me," I say. My voice is serious and she nods her head.

"Whatever you want," she says, as I knew she would.

She kisses me and bites my bottom lip which makes the hair on the back of my neck stand up. I feel her drift away. Her long eyelashes flutter from her dreaming. She doesn't have nightmares anymore.

Aiya isn't very tall but her legs are long. Not wanting to wake her up I let her straddle me even though it means I won't be able to sleep. I think of spiders and centipedes. Unable to close my eyes I notice the weight of her on my chest as I imagine a hundred arms and legs holding me.

***

Chiyo and Haru invite us over for tea. I sit next to Yuta. He and his sister both have appealing facial features making them stand out. Haru sits next to her husband and I catch her glancing in my direction.

"So, Chiyo. Anyone special in your life?" asks Aiya with a wide grin.

"Kind of," giggles Chiyo. She is twirling her shoulder length hair in between her fingers.

"She won't tell us!" says Haru. Her voice reminds me of the ring of a bell.

"Can you believe it? My twin sister is keeping secrets from me," jokes Yuta.

"A lady never kisses and tells," teases Chiyo. She sticks her tongue out at her brother.

"Is he handsome?" asks Haru. She stares into the teacup and blushes.

"Yes," says Chiyo. She is somewhere else. Her ocean eyes are days away.

"Do I know him?" asks Aiya.

I wish I had more to add to the conversation but I'm groggy from my lack of sleep and distracted by the memory of her legs around me.

"You do. I will tell you all one day. I'm not ready right now," whispers Chiyo. Everyone nods and changes the subject.

"Riku, how does it feel to be back in the village?" asks Yuta.

"It's nice to be back," I say.

This answer pleases Aiya and she rests her head on my shoulder. Haru is staring at me like she wants to say something but I keep my gaze down. The girl with dimples and magic hair makes me sheepish.

"Aiya, you look more beautiful than ever. It's so good to see you smile," says Chiyo in her singsong voice.

"Thank you. I've never been happier," says Aiya. She is genuine.

"How long have you two been in love?" asks Haru. Her chestnut eyes bore into me and I feel my rib cage constrict.

"For a long time." Aiya speaks for both of us.

"Riku, you saved Aiya many years ago. Did you know you loved her then?" The young girl's question creates a lump in my throat.

"Not that night. Three summers after we met I heard her sing about me. That's when I fell in love with her," I admit.

"That's such a romantic story," says Haru as she touches her heart and smiles. Yuta hugs her and kisses the top of her head.

"I almost didn't propose to Haru. After you defeated the centipede I had the courage to finally ask her to marry me. Thank you, Riku," says Yuta.

He looks at me with sincere gratitude. His wife looks at me like I am a god. I never thought my actions could affect others in such a way.

"It's getting late. We better get going," says Aiya. I agree and our friends wave us out. The stars are shining and we stop to admire them. One of them shoots across the sky and we both gasp. Aiya looks at me like she has witnessed a miracle.

"I love you," I say it first.

"I love you." She kisses me and we continue walking. "Do you ever wish on the stars?" she asks.

"I don't have to. You are my girl, the one with stars on her face."

"I wished for us to be together forever," she says.

"Don't worry. We will be."

"You promise?"

"I promise," I say.

"It's okay if one day you don't love me anymore. I won't be mad." What Aiya says shocks me and I grab her wrist and stop us in our tracks.

"Why would you say that?" I ask.

"It's just that I love you so much. I wouldn't want you to stay with me if you were unhappy."

"I'll always love you. I should have come back for you sooner. Please, don't think I would ever stop loving you."

"If you had one wish what would it be?"

"I'd wish to go back in time. The day I heard your song about me. I'd go back and kiss you. Seeing you cry as you sang still haunts me," I say.

"It's okay, Riku. I'm glad we met the way we did."

"You are?"

"Yes. My journey to find you taught me a lot. I learned to believe in myself and have faith in you. You heard me call your name and you came running. I think that's when we were destined to meet again."

I contemplate what Aiya is saying for a while. The stars spill across the indigo tapestry in the sky. I'm uncertain but I think the gods are watching.

"I think so, too." Once we're in Aiya's house she lights the fire and we get into bed.

"Riku, can I ask you a question?"

"What is it?"

"You told me about your brother Ryo and your sisters Yuri and Yama. Do you have any other siblings?" she asks.

"Yes. My sister Rena is the eldest and most vicious. She should have been queen but my father was against the idea of a female leader. My baby brother Yahei betrayed me after I fled the challenge. He let Ryo manipulate him after he became king."

"What makes everyone so cruel?"

"It's the demonic canon. Wolf demons follow the word of an ancient book. Our religion asks us to destroy and take. It wants us to subdue others with our strength. War is a necessity because of our greed and need to rule. There is never enough gold, silk, or power."

"You're not a believer?"

"No. I never believed that the king was god," I say.

"What do you know about the wolf god?"

"Very little. My sister Yama was our spiritual leader. It's vague but her teachings said the wolf god was angered by humanity's increasing disrespect towards the forest. I was told he retreated into the spectral plain where he rules the mountains from beyond the moon."

"Do the gods speak to you?" she asks.

"I spoke to a demigod. His name was Satoru."

"What did he say?" Her question pushes the breath from my lungs and the words escape me.

"He said you and I would be together for centuries." I don't want to mention Kasai's name. My answer is honest enough.

"Did he really?"

"Yes, really. The gods' messenger brought me to you. I found your village because a white deer led me there," I confess. I've never told Aiya any of this. Her eyes are wide.

"I had a dream about a white deer once. The night before my sixteenth birthday. I saw it in the treeline next to the camphors and hydrangeas. There was someone in the forest with it but I couldn't see who it was. That morning I paced by the oaks and camphors outside the village for hours. I heard a twig snap and I thought someone was watching me."

"That was me," I say.

"You were just out of my reach," she says and she touches my face. We are nose to nose.

"I'm sorry."

"Don't be. I like our love story just the way it is."

***

I plan on proposing to Aiya on her twentieth birthday. It seems wrong to be someone's whole world when they are so young. I've been alive for over two centuries. I want Aiya to have more of her life for herself. I know she wants everything right now but I insist on waiting.

She is twirling around, catching snowflakes in her hair, and melting the ice. Today she's wearing the yellow kimono, reminding me of the day I first heard her sing about me. It has orange floral designs and a green obi. She is my endless summer. Her smile fades.

"What is it?" I ask.

"Riku, do you hear that?" Her pretty face becomes grave and her eyes search in every direction. I stop and listen. Low grunting mixed with squeaking.

"It's a troop of monkey demons," I say. Aiya's face becomes solemn and I can tell she's afraid.

"What do we do?" she asks.

"Stay next to me."

The tree branches vibrate and snow is shaken from the pines. Acorns and pinecones hit the ground. The leader of the monkey demons speaks.

"Well, well, well. What do we have here?" he says.

The demon monkey king wears a gold crown and purple trousers. His staff is gold and has the head of a snake on it. The serpent's eyes are iridescent emeralds.

"Leave us be!" I bark. I keep Aiya behind me and hold onto her hand.

"Look, boys. He has something real pretty with him," says the monkey king. I growl at him and the smaller monkey demons retreat into the higher branches.

"Don't even think about it," I say.

My canines are bared and I can't contain the raspy rumble in my throat. Glancing over my shoulder I see Aiya stare at the monkey king with that unreadable expression. She doesn't seem afraid anymore.

"We were searching for some persimmons but I see you have something much sweeter. Get her, boys!" demands the monkey king. Ten of the demons leap from the trees and land in a circle around us. I draw my sword and pull Aiya next to me.

"She's even prettier up close," says one of the demons as he licks his lips.

"She smells good, too. Like honey," spits another. I feel the rage build up in me.

"Back off!" I growl. The monkey demons carry gold batons. They draw their prestigious weapons with jeweled fingers. Their extreme wealth repulses me. The biggest one has shiny purple trousers and a red vest.

"Oh, come on! We'll give her back when we're done," taunts the goliath monkey demon. My veins wither as my blood spoils.

"You'll have to pry her from my cold, dead hands," I say and prepare myself to murder them.

They all charge at once. Saliva drips from their fangs. They screech and hiss. The sound is disgusting. I'm about to swing my blade in a wide circle but a tall fire barrier is put up, preventing the monkey demons from approaching us. My arms relax and I let go of Aiya, admiring the flames.

"How did you do that?" I ask.

"I've been practicing," she says.

Aiya smiles at me. The fire in her eyes burns but it ignites something beautiful inside her. We stay in the safety of her flames and marvel at her new abilities. She puts down the fire barrier. The monkey demons are gone.

"You did it, Aiya. You protected us," I pick her up and kiss her.

"I did, didn't I?"

Aiya seems proud of herself. She is smiling but I feel hurt. I realize it's because Aiya doesn't need me anymore.

CHAPTER FOUR

A Thousand Smiles

I take the gold button off my undershirt. There's two more on the collar of my bodysuit and I tear those off as well. Studying them closely I see our insignia and the words "Nothing without you." Aiya is still asleep. I whisper to her I'll be right back. She can't hear me but I feel better telling her anyway.

Once I'm outside the shops I begin to feel nervous. I felt confident this morning but now I'm wondering if I'm being foolish. I decide to go into the swordsmith shop. I haven't spoken to Hajime since we arrived and I should be more polite. Entering the shop I'm hit with the scent of sweat, metal, and ash.

"Riku! I heard you and Aiya were back." Hajime steps out to greet me. He bows to me and I bow back. I am most formal with him.

"Yes. It's nice to see you." I am sincere but I feel a grudge growing in the back of my mind.

"It's so good to see you. How is Aiya?" he asks. His violet eyes shimmer and I feel myself becoming jealous.

"She's happy," I say.

"Good. I've always wanted Aiya to be happy," he says with no malice or envy.

"I have a request, Hajime."

"What is it?" he looks at me perplexed. I hold out the buttons to him.

"I want someone to make these into a ring for her." Hajime picks up a button and examines it with care.

"What does this mean, 'Nothing without you.'"

"It's from our people's demonic canon." Reflexively I put two fingers to my lips before pointing at him. Hajime nods his head to show he understands.

"These are real gold. It must have cost a lot to make these. Each one would be individually poured and embellished with the symbol." He says this because he's interested but I feel awkward about him looking into my past.

"My people are incredibly wealthy," I admit.

"I can make the ring for her," he says.

"You can?"

"Yes. I'm not just a swordsmith. I can make almost anything out of precious metals," he says and his smile causes creases in the corners of his eyes. I want to say "no" but Aiya told me Hajime was her friend. He knows her better than I. He loved her first. I pull out a pouch of coins and hand it to him.

"Thank you, Hajime."

"I don't want your money. I would do anything for Aiya." His words cut through me.

"Are you sure?" I ask.

"Yes, I'm sure. I can have it ready for you in three days."

"I appreciate it," I say.

"It's no problem. It brings me happiness to make something so wonderful. Thank you for asking me. It means a lot."

"I'll see you in three days."

"See you then. Bye, Riku." He waves at me like I'm his friend. I shouldn't be but I am envious of his ability to love her without jealousy or possessiveness.

***

It's been snowing nonstop. I love it though. Aiya doesn't mind the cold and we weave through the cedars and ferns together. She spies a red deer and begins chasing after it. It reminds me of Hoshi and I get a burning sickness in my stomach. By the time she returns I've shaken off the memory.

"Are you okay, Riku?" asks Aiya.

"I'm fine. Just enjoying the snow."

I look up into the gray and white sky to let the snowflakes land in my eyelashes and rest in my hair. A flying squirrel chirps at us and Aiya makes small noises back at it. To my amazement the tiny creature flies from the branch he is on and lands on her shoulder. Aiya picks him up and strokes the spot between its ears. It looks at me with beady black eyes.

"Look, Riku! He likes me," she giggles. The squirrel scurries up her arm and onto her shoulder where he hides in her hair. He peeks out at me from behind her neck. Aiya's sweetness towards the animal fills my heart and it weighs heavy in my chest. I reach out and touch her freckles.

"Who wouldn't like you?"

My question makes her smile. She kisses my cheek and runs off again. I know she wants me to play with her so I give chase. Her dark blue kimono reminds me of stormy skies. Ink black tresses sway back and forth in front of me. She is my summer, my ocean, my stars. I try to grab her arm but she changes directions and I lose her.

"Aiya!" I call her name a few more times. Her squirrel friend jumps on my shoulder from one of the cedars. "Hey, little guy. Where did she go?" I ask him. He tilts his head and hops on top of my head.

"He likes you," Aiya's voice hangs in the air above me. I look up and she knocks me into the snow. Her little friend chirps at us and runs off.

"Why do you always hide from me?"

She's straddling me again and I attempt to push her off me without seeming rude.

"I'm not hiding. I would never hide from you. I'm just playing." Her deep dark eyes gaze into my soul as she holds my shoulders. "I think you are the one who tends to hide from me," she says. Her words shred through me like the boar demon's tusks.

"I'm sorry. I don't mean to," I say.

"I know you need your space. I try not to bother you about it but I get scared you're not going to come back." I can't take it anymore and I pull Aiya on top of me and watch snow dance around her hair and stick in the ink.

"I would never leave you. Never." Snowflakes fall from the sky and blur my vision but I don't get up or move her.

"You promise?" she asks.

"I promise," I say. We lay in the white powder and listen to the haunting song of the cranes. I want this moment to last forever.

"Let's go home."

She helps me sit up and brushes the snow off my shoulders. I agree and she pulls me through the forest back to the village. My favorite color on her is yellow but not just any yellow, yellow like buttercups.

Today my favorite color on her is blue. She looks like a storm or a dream. Aiya is the ocean I would drown in. I let her lure me into the depths of the sea. She makes me jasmine and green tea, it's her favorite. I've been learning about Aiya and all of her favorites. There's a lot to remember but I want to know everything about her. She prefers to get up early. I like to sleep late.

She looks good in everything but her favorite kimono is red. It has black flowers on it. The spider lily hairsticks she wears were a present from her mother. She hasn't said much about her father. His weakness gnaws at her. We sit outside and look at the waxing crescent moon. The stars reflect in her scarlet eyes and I see her watching the world.

"What are you thinking about?" I ask her. She keeps her gaze on the sky.

"I was wondering if the wolf god could see us now," she says.

"I have wondered that for many years."

"Riku, what do you believe in?"

"I'm not sure. For a long time I thought I didn't believe in anything. The truth is I couldn't believe in a book that told me to kill my father."

"I thought I was no one but I have been everything. All the changes I've gone through have caused me to question what it means to have faith."

"What do you mean?" I ask.

"When I was searching for you I began to lose hope. Brother Minoru said to me, 'Have faith, Aiya. Faith is what keeps us alive.' There were days I thought I would die alone in the forest but I repeated what he told me in my head. Over and over. It was what I was thinking when I called your name," she says.

"Were you a nonbeliever?" I ask.

"Yes. After I woke up and saw you I knew someone was watching over me. I have believed ever since."

"Someone is. The demigod told me so."

I look over to see her rosy mouth stretched across her face. She gets up and I follow her back inside. Out of the corner of my eye I see Aiya throw her stormy kimono onto the floor and get into bed. Her ring should be done tomorrow. It's still another six months until her birthday but I want everything to be perfect.

"Riku?" her husky voice is muffled by the pillow. I get into bed with her and she clings to me like she'll never see me again.

"What's wrong?" I ask.

"Nothing. I just want you close to me."

Slender arms with stars on them wrap around me. I cover her up with the blanket and close my eyes. My fingertips caress her spine. Resting my chin on the top of her head I fall into a blissful sleep.

I wake up to her pulling at the collar of my shirt and kissing my neck again. I pretend to be asleep but she doesn't stop. Now I'm distracted and my breaths are shallow.

"Please, don't."

"Sorry," she says. Aiya stops but I can't go back to sleep. I kiss the top of her head and try to think about the forest, rivers, and mountains. Anything to drown out the improper thoughts.

"It's okay," I whisper. I am drifting in and out but she's biting my bottom lip and I feel her tongue in my mouth. "Stop!" I don't mean to but I bark at her. She retreats inside herself. I feel guilty.

"I love you," she says.

"I love you, too."

She makes me crazy. I try to go back to sleep. Focused on other things I listen to the wind move through the trees around us. Somehow I fade out. I dream about proposing to her. How happy I know she will be. I smile in my sleep thinking about it.

Her long leg wrapped around me stirs me awake. I open my eyes to see the stars on her collarbone. Closing them I attempt to dull the sight from my mind. At first I think I'm dreaming but then I realize Aiya's singing.

* * *

The wolf was once lonely
But never again
He is my one
He is my only

Something breaks in me and I kiss her so hard I worry it will frighten her. She doesn't reject me and kisses me back. I almost wish she wouldn't because I can't control myself anymore. Her hand is on my chest, my hands are in her hair, and her tongue is in my mouth. I give into her even though it feels like I'm betraying us both.

***

Morning is here and it brings light to what we did in the dark. At first I feel hollow and strange. That is until Aiya wakes up and smiles at me. I smile every time she smiles. She covers my face in a hundred kisses and I have to beg her to stop.

"I can't breathe."

"Sorry." She is always saying she's sorry to me.

"Don't say that."

"What?"

"That you're sorry," I say.

"Why?" she asks. Aiya's childish line of asking questions hits me in the heart but it doesn't hurt.

"Because you never have to say you're sorry to me. Okay?"

"Okay."

She kisses the tip of my nose and closes her eyes. I want to get up but I can't stop looking at her. Her long eyelashes remind me of butterfly wings. They flutter as she dreams. Taking her hair in my palm and twisting it around my wrist I feel content. Aiya's kissing my neck again. This time I don't resist her and I give in right away. Maybe I should have got up when she fell back asleep.

"I'll be right back," I say.

"Where are you going?" she asks.

"It's going to be a surprise."

"I like surprises."

Aiya makes no effort to get out of bed. She rests her head on my side of the bed and waves goodbye to me. I love her so much but I am relieved to be by myself for a minute. How the pangs of guilt pierce through me.

I gave into her not once but twice. The sky is cloudy and I wonder if the gods look down at me with disdain. Aiya has been my everything but now I know I will be her everything. It doesn't matter if I don't feel up to the challenge, I have to take it.

I arrive at Hajime's shop and see two people waiting inside. Feeling awkward I choose to wait outside and catch my breath. Everything is different but not. I wonder why I felt hollow upon my waking. Being in love confuses me.

"Riku?" It's Hajime.

"Hey."

"It's ready. I hope she likes it. I made it custom. Look," he says and urges me to inspect his work. There's a slight trembling in my palm as he hands it to me. It's excellently crafted. I hold it up to get a closer look at it and I see the engraving on the inside.

"Nothing without you," I say out loud without meaning to.

"I hope you don't mind. I thought it was too sentimental to erase." Hajime is an authentic and respectable person. If he thinks she will like it, she will like it.

"It's perfect. Thank you, Hajime."

"You're welcome." He smiles at the ring in my hand. I wonder if he can see the tremor.

"I was going to wait but I want to ask her soon," I say. My announcement causes Hajime to chuckle.

"Why would you wait?" he asks.

"I don't know. I want it to be special."

"No matter when or how you ask it will be special to her. Aiya is going to be really happy. You shouldn't keep her waiting." I clutch the ring and feel the shape of it against my fingers.

"You're right. She deserves to be happy," I say. Hajime puts his hand on my shoulder.

"She already is. But this will make her smile a thousand smiles in a single moment. Be ready for that moment. Don't forget her face when you ask her," he says. The weight of his hand is gone and he continues to hammer out steel while I grind through the metal in my thoughts.

***

"Are you ready?" I ask. She nods and I tie my obi around her eyes. I pick her up and I dash through the forest, shredding the moss off the bark, and run with her like the first time we met. The sky is blue today. There are no clouds.

"Riku, where are we going?"

"I told you, it's a surprise."

"I like surprises," she says. Aiya is beautiful but her voice is my weakness.

"Do you trust me?" I ask her.

"Yes."

She doesn't hesitate for a second. I jump into the ravine. She clings to me but I make sure to shield her with my cloak and I land on my feet. The crater in the gorge kicks up the mud from beneath the snow. We are in the gulley and I notice shadows above me. I look up to see two cranes.

Slowing down I hear a chirp from the cedars. It's Aiya's little squirrel friend. Aiya can sing to the birds and they sing back. The spirits of the forest admire her. I've seen them peek at her from boulders and tree stumps. Everyone loves her. I wonder how I am so lucky. It scares me at times to think about being the one she loves.

She's wearing the yellow kimono today. Summer in the harshest winter. Aiya can unfreeze an icy heart. She is able to accept the hurt life has dealt her. Somehow she is strong enough to withstand forgiving over and over again. I set her down.

"Keep your eyes closed," I say. She smiles and nods. I take the blindfold off. Her eyelashes are so long they touch the stars on her face.

"Can I open them now?" she asks. I don't want this moment to end. I hold her shoulders and turn her around.

"Okay. You can open them now," I say. Aiya gasps and covers her mouth.

"Riku, how did you find this place?"

"I wanted to find somewhere special for you."

She smiles at me and I feel my heart burst in my chest. Aiya takes off and begins to run through the endless field of peonies and roses. I looked everywhere to find the perfect place. The peonies paint the hillsides pink and purple. White and blue roses line the perimeter of the valley.

I chase after her as I know she wants me to. She thinks she's out of my reach but I sneak up on her right and grab her. I swing her around, fanning her black hair out. She hands me a blue rose and kisses me.

"It's beautiful here," she sighs.

"Nothing and no one is as beautiful as you, though."

"Really?"

"Yes, really," I say and take her hand.

We walk through the winter peonies going on for miles. Aiya begins braiding her hair, weaving in the pink and purple flowers. The curtain of black ink is adorned with many blossoms when she's done. She is my forever summer in yellow, my storm, my ocean in blue. Aiya is the embers of my heart in red.

"I've been wanting to ask you something."

She stops walking but continues to play with her hair.

"What is it?" Her question forces the air from my lungs.

I want to remember her like this. Aiya, in her yellow kimono with flowers in her hair, looking at me as though I am the only person in the world. I get on one knee and pull out the ring Hajime made for her.

"Aiya, will you marry me?"

I'm disappointed she doesn't smile right away like I thought she would. Instead she stares at the ring and then me. Maybe Hajime was wrong. Perhaps marrying me wouldn't make her happy. Aiya is eye level with me when I kneel and her deep mystifying gaze leaves her thoughts a mystery to me.

Her embrace is so sudden, so fierce, it nearly knocks the wind out of me. I feel tears on her face and I'm worried I did something wrong. Aiya leans into me and whispers in my ear.

"I've been waiting for you to ask me," she says. Aiya gives a small laugh but she's still crying. My heart breaks and I cry when she cries.

"How long have you been waiting?" I ask.

"Since my sixteenth birthday," she says. I pull back to study her face. She's serious.

"Would you have said yes to me then? I would have been a stranger to you."

"I didn't think of you as a stranger. I saw you every night in my dreams." I kiss her and she pushes me into the snow. Putting her hand up we both admire the ring on her finger.

"I know what I would wish for," I say. Aiya looks at me surprised.

"What?"

"For this moment to last forever," I say. Then it happens. Aiya gives me a smile that's worth a thousand smiles.

CHAPTER FIVE

Fear is the Opposite of Faith

Since I've proposed to Aiya I try my best to not leave her alone for very long. I seldom take off on my own but when I do I come back much sooner than I usually would. I don't want her to worry. She doesn't tell me what I can and can't do but I know my disappearing upsets her. Nothing is worth more than her happiness.

Aiya doesn't ask anything of me and I feel lost as to what I should do most of the time. More often than not she is the one who takes care of us. Living alone in the forest has left many defects in my personality. I spend the time I'm lost in my head analyzing Aiya and attempt to predict what she wants, what she needs. Anytime I ask her she says she wants me to be happy. It makes me crazy.

I give into her all the time now. Everything has changed. I didn't plan on proposing to her until summer and it's midwinter. There are days where I think it's better like this but then there are other times I worry I have betrayed us both. I look down at Aiya and see she is cuddling her little squirrel friend. He allows her to touch his nose with hers.

"What's his name?" I ask her. She smiles and looks into his eyes for a moment. She lights up when she decides.

"His name is Niko." The squirrel perks up at his name. Aiya can charm anybody, beast, human, or demon. Niko scurries up her kimono and hides in her hair. This makes her giggle. I find myself smiling more.

"Everyone loves you. How am I so lucky to be the one you love?"

"I am the lucky one," she says.

Aiya reaches into her hair and pulls out Niko. She hands him to me. The squirrel seems frightened but I can tell he trusts Aiya. She doesn't know her affect on those around her.

"Do you really think so?" I ask. We continue walking back to Aiya's house and it starts to snow. She is having fun melting the snowflakes on her tongue.

"I love you. I wouldn't lie to you."

She keeps dancing. Niko and I watch her with longing stares. I am careful not to scare her squirrel friend. We are both captivated by Aiya and the way she makes us feel important. Aiya holds out her hands and I give Niko back to her. She kisses him on top of his furry head. I didn't know it was possible but I think the little creature is blushing under his fur. He looks at me and then back at her before he flies back into the cedars. This makes Aiya laugh and I pick her up. I love her laugh. It's almost as intoxicating as her singing.

"I love you," I say it to her first everyday now.

She kisses me and holds onto me until we get to her house. Once we're home she starts the fire and I get into bed. She brushes her hair. I admire the shiny black ink running down her back. In a way I am jealous of Aiya's squirrel friend because he can hide in there.

Being with Aiya isn't difficult but I'm exhausted from the constant company. I don't want to be alone but I crave time to myself. Aiya doesn't come to bed but I can hear her behind me. The sound of boiling water and the scent of jasmine green tea lulls me to sleep.

It seems too good to be true and I think I'm dreaming but I'm not. Aiya is pressed against me with my hand on her heart. The beating beneath my palm is soothing but it's the ring on her finger that causes me to look again just to be sure it's real. I lift up her hair and kiss her neck. Even though it's winter I am never cold because Aiya is never cold.

"Are you awake?" she asks.

"Yes." She turns to face me and kisses my nose. It reminds me of her squirrel friend and makes me smile. This makes Aiya smile.

"Riku, do you like surprises?" I think about her question. The entire time I lived in the northern mountains my life was predictable and planned out for me. Only after I left did I begin to experience surprises.

It was rough in the beginning but as the years went by I looked forward to learning new things about people, demons, and myself. The chaos was exciting to me. Aiya is by far the biggest surprise in my life and I love her more than anything.

"Yes," I say. Aiya opens her kimono and takes my hand. She places it on the stars below her navel. It's subtle but I feel the slight pulse of something alive. Startled, I pull my hand back a bit too harshly. Aiya looks hurt and sits up.

"I'm sorry. I thought you would be happy," she says. The sadness in her voice is unbearable. I reach for her and put my hand back on the stars on her stomach.

"I am happy. I just wasn't expecting this so soon is all. Come here."

I pull her down next to me and keep my hand on her starry skin. "Don't say sorry. Especially about this." She puts her hand over mine and my heart flutters when I feel the ring on her finger and the quiver of my baby inside her.

***

It's almost the middle of the night but I get up anyway. Aiya wakes up early and I don't want her to reach for me and feel I'm not there. I throw on my clothes and my boots. Sneaking out the door I take another look at her. She's sleeping soundly with her left hand below her navel.

I don't plan on being out for very long. Just enough time to get some air. I had to place my hand on the smoothness of Aiya's stomach to make sure what she told me wasn't a dream. Everything is moving faster and faster. I expected this but not so early into our relationship. At first I'm angry with myself for giving into her but then I realize what is really bothering me. I'm angry that I'm afraid.

My father was a coldhearted warmonger. What does that make me? I worry I'll be a terrible father. Aiya's father betrayed her. I can't fail her. She means too much to me. The forest is dark but I can see. It doesn't matter because I am too lost inside myself to pay attention to what's going on around me. A twig breaks to my left, pulling me out of my thoughts. I look over and see her. It's the white deer. I haven't seen her since I spoke with Satoru. She approaches me with caution and stares at me with otherworldly eyes.

"Hey." I don't know what to say to the white deer. Kneeling down to get a better look into her eyes I see the reflection of the gods. They do not look at me with disdain. We gaze into each other's souls and I sense that she is telling me everything's okay. "Thank you," I say. She bounds away and I feel relieved.

The sun isn't up yet. I make my way back to Aiya's house. She's still asleep. I crawl back into bed with her and put my hand on the stars below her navel. The slight stir inside makes my heart race and I scorn my cowardice. I look at Aiya sleeping. Her face is relaxed and she smiles in her sleep. How is she so brave?

***

There is snow on the ground but Hanako should be here in a few weeks time. Aiya has told most of our friends about her pregnancy but is most excited to share it with Hanako. I am at a loss for words and let Aiya do the talking for both of us. Natsume, Hiromi, and Daina shrieked with joy and rubbed her belly profusely. Brother Minoru cried as I expected he would and Lady Kiyori remained calm but I could tell she wanted to say more. The priestesses stare at me as I stand behind Aiya and let her share our wonderful news. I feel protective and hold her close to my side but have little to say.

Aiya has been waiting to share with Chiyo. I am not sure why. We are heading to Hajime's shop where we are supposed to meet them. Aiya's left hand never leaves her stomach. After Aiya told me she was pregnant I began to notice how it changed her. She smells different. The honey and tea leaves is now tinged with a milky scent. It's not bad but I miss the way it was before. Her face is flushed and the stars on her face seem lighter. I convince myself that just because things are changing doesn't mean they're bad.

"Riku! Aiya," exclaims Chiyo. She's waiting outside the shop for us. Her ocean blue eyes and berry lips stand out against the white and gray.

"Hi Chiyo," I say. I feel more comfortable around Chiyo than any of Aiya's other friends. Chiyo embraces her, taking a lock of her hair, and twirls it in her fingers.

"What did you want to tell me?" she asks.

The girl with the widow's peak has a high voice but it's not shrill like Hiromi or Daina's. Hajime steps outside to join us, wiping the sweat from his brow. He smells like steel and embers.

"Aiya, Riku! How are you?" asks Hajime.

"Never been better," says Aiya.

There's a twinge in my chest and I don't know why.

"You said you had something to tell us."

Hajime looks up at me and I feel ashamed. If he was in my situation he wouldn't be going through what I'm going through. Chiyo smiles at me and it's like a punch to the throat. What is wrong with me?

"I'm pregnant," she says. Aiya smiles.

I look to Hajime first to gauge his reaction. His jaw drops but I can tell he is genuinely happy for her. He looks to Chiyo and they both stare down at Aiya's stomach, covered by the hand with the ring on it. Chiyo jumps and claps the way I imagine Hanako will.

"That's great news! Congratulations! You two must be so happy," says Chiyo. She has her hands clasped to her chest. I know she wants to be married and have a child. Somehow she is able to be happy for Aiya and me with no indication of envy. It pains me to look right at her and see the joy paint her face.

"It brings me happiness to see you two start your family," says Hajime. I know he is telling the truth and it makes me resent him.

"Riku, what do you want to name your baby?" asks Chiyo.

"I want Aiya to pick their name," I say. Aiya kisses me and it eases me a bit.

"I'm not sure yet. It will come to me," says Aiya. This makes Chiyo and Hajime happy. Aiya named her squirrel friend and he liked it. I know Aiya picked her baby brother's name. She should be the one to name our child.

"Riku, do you want a boy or a girl?" asks Hajime. The question annoys me but I am polite.

"I just want them to be healthy and happy." Aiya likes my answer and she embraces me. It melts my heart and I loosen my grasp on her.

"You will all be happy," says Hajime. He reaches for Aiya's stomach. To my horror Aiya takes his hand and places it where the stars are. The place where I touch her. I don't realize it at first but everyone is staring at me. It's because I have a low growl in my throat.

"Sorry," I mumble. Chiyo puts her hand on Aiya as well and the three of them ignore my rude behavior. I'm sure Aiya will scold me later.

"Wow," whispers Hajime.

"What?" I ask. My body is tense and I want to leave.

"It's just so beautiful," he says. Chiyo holds his shoulders and they both smile at Aiya's belly.

"We better get going. I'll see you two tomorrow. Goodbye!"

Aiya waves to them and I do, too. My throat is scratchy from the growling. I swallow and keep my mouth shut. Aiya doesn't seem upset or annoyed with me. She holds my hand the whole way to her house, her other hand feeling the pulse of her pregnancy. When we get home she gets into bed and I stay up.

"Riku, are you going to come to bed?" she asks.

"In a little bit. I have a lot on my mind," I say.

"Okay."

Aiya closes her eyes and I wait for her to fall asleep. I shine my armor and clean my

boots. I wash my face and clean my teeth. There is no way I can sleep tonight. My head is in a hundred different places. After doing every task I can think of I get into bed with Aiya. She is always warm but tonight she feels burning hot. I ignore it and fall asleep wondering about what it means to be a husband. What does it mean to be a father?

CHAPTER SIX

All the Blood I Lost with You

"Riku?" I didn't think I would be able to go to sleep but I wake up to Aiya saying my name. Her voice is shaky. I sit up right away.

"What's wrong?"

I open my eyes to see Aiya's hair sticking to the sweat on her face. She has tears cascading from her eyes and she looks terrified. It hits me so hard it makes my nose twitch. I smell blood. Aiya pulls back the blanket and I see why she is crying. There is blood running down her legs, staining her thighs, and the white sheets.

"Riku, I'm really scared," she says. I don't want to tell her that I am more afraid than she is. The tremor in my hand has returned.

"It's okay. I'm here," I say with false confidence. I wrap her in the blanket and pick her up. The memory of the night we met pops into my mind.

"What should we do?" Aiya is sobbing. Lifting her up I see the blood has soaked the mat as well.

"I'm going to get you some help."

I make sure she is covered up and we exit her house and enter the snowy atmosphere. Aiya is crying into my neck. I'm not sure what to do or who to talk to but I end up at Lady Kiyori's house. I knock on the door twice.

"What's wrong?" she asks.

The priestess looks at me and then to Aiya sobbing in my arms. The blood drips from the blanket and tints the snow scarlet. Lady

Kiyori is able to communicate without words and ushers us inside. I set Aiya down but refuse to let go of her. The priestess grabs a bowl of hot water and towels. She pulls the blanket away from Aiya and I feel embarrassed about Lady Kiyori seeing us like this. The priestess shows no signs of annoyance or judgment. I can tell she cares. Aiya is too upset to talk so I speak for us this time.

"Aiya woke up like this," I say. The priestess feels Aiya's feverish face and her forehead creases.

"Has she shown any indication of sickness? Complaints of any pain?" she asks. I look at Aiya and she shakes her head "no."

"Last night she felt warmer than usual."

"Aiya, have you been feeling distressed or overwhelmed?" asks the priestess. Aiya shakes her head "no" profusely.

"No, I've been really happy," she cries. Her answer causes her to cry more. It breaks my heart and I cry with her. Lady Kiyori continues to clean the blood off of Aiya with a straight face. I cling onto Aiya and I worry I am holding her too tight but I can't let go.

"Riku, are you okay?" asks the priestess.

"I'm okay."

The priestess stops her work to look at me for a moment. It makes me uncomfortable so I bury my face in Aiya's hair. Lady Kiyori pours hot water into a cup with an herbal concoction and gives it to Aiya. It smells like winterberries and citrus.

"Here, it will make you feel better," says the priestess.

Aiya sips on the drink as Lady Kiyori throws out the bloody water and begins washing the towels. I'm not sure the intended effect of the tea but Aiya relaxes and drifts away.

"She's asleep," I announce. The priestess stops what she's doing and kneels down across from us. I want to hide my face in Aiya's hair but I don't.

"May I?" Lady Kiyori gestures towards Aiya's stomach. I nod my head and the priestess presses the stars of Aiya's navel with caution. She massages the skin and uses the tips of her fingers to trace the constellations.

"Is she going to be okay?" I speak into the back of Aiya's head. Her hair is wet with my tears. The priestess gives me a reassuring smile.

"Aiya and your baby will be okay," she says.

"Are you sure?" As soon as I ask, the priestess takes my hand and places it on Aiya's navel. It's less noticeable but there is the faint pulse of something alive below the surface. I feel myself fill with relief and let out a sigh.

"Aiya's body has been through a lot of changes. She is strong, so is your baby. But she needs to rest for a few days. Make sure she doesn't strain herself. I know you will take good care of her."

"I will," I say.

"And as much fun as she's having, don't let her dance in the snow or jump from the trees for a while. Okay?"

"I don't think Aiya will like me telling her what to do." This makes Lady Kiyori laugh and it's striking. I've never heard her so much as giggle.

"I'm sure she won't. She didn't like when I told her what to do either."

"What was Aiya like growing up?" I ask. The question escapes my lips. I didn't mean to ask but it's too late. The priestess looks at Aiya sleeping and her face softens.

"She was a sad girl. Very lonely even though she didn't need to be. Chiyo opened her heart but she remained distant from us until her transformation."

"Really?" I ask.

"Aiya couldn't see how loved she was until recently," says Lady Kiyori. The priestess looks into my eyes and I feel her searching through my soul. I'm worried what she will find. Her gaze is deep and mystifying like Aiya's.

"But everyone loves her." More tears spill out but I don't feel ashamed in front of the priestess anymore.

"Aiya didn't love herself. She does now." I pull Aiya to my chest as close as I can without hurting her. Aiya seemed depressed when I first met her. Ever since Kasai changed her she's been playful and lively. Sometimes I forget Aiya has a past, too.

"I love her so much it's unbearable," I confess.

The priestess gives me a serious glance. She scoots next to me and puts her hand on my back and uses the other to pull long black tresses out of Aiya's face.

"Love is painful, Riku. It is the strongest force in the world. We can fight it but the heart wants what the heart wants. Aiya waited for you all those years and I told her to forget about you. I thought it was just a girlish fantasy she had. I am so sorry I said those things. You don't know me but I hope you believe me when I say that Aiya has loved you since I met her. She never stopped waiting for your return." The priestess's admission causes me to succumb to my sadness. My tears soak Aiya's hair and today I am her storm, I am the rain.

***

Lady Kiyori gave me a container of the winterberry and citrus tea. I'm supposed to give it to Aiya twice a day. The drink makes her tired and she sleeps a majority of the time. Thinking of what the priestess said and the memory of Hajime touching Aiya's starry skin urges me to take better care of her. I vow to be a good husband and father. We won't be like my family.

Aiya is the one who washes our clothes and feeds us but right now I'm the one who will need to take care of us. I chide myself on how unhelpful I've been in the past. It's easier for me to fight armies of boar demons than to do daily chores. Not anymore though, I will change. I will be a better man.

I head to the river and wash Aiya's blood out of the sheets. Inky clouds of red float downstream. I've never done anything like this. During my years as a soldier and a prince I had servants to do everything for me. The years I spent alone I took care of myself but it's completely different than being responsible for another person. Remembering what brought on the blood, the baby, I get a pressure against my sternum knowing I will be responsible for not just one but two people.

I go up river until I see plentiful fish. Crouching down I stare into the running water and the swimming silver bodies. I swipe them out of the icy liquid with my claws. Feeling satisfied with my catch I head back towards Aiya's house.

"Well, aren't you sweet." It's that damn cat again.

"Back off!" I bark.

"What? I mean it! I think it's endearing how much you love that little mouse."

"Go away," I shoo him and keep walking but he follows and snow falls from the branches he lands on.

"I can smell her blood. Is she alright?" he asks. The tiger demon isn't smirking or laughing.

"Why? Do you care?"

"I am intrigued by her. I remember her looking for you. You should be flattered by my interest," he says.

"Really now? Flattered?" I spit. The corner of the tiger demon's lips turn up.

"Yes. I see lots of demons. I know all the happenings in this part of the forest. I see everything and I have never seen two people fated to be together the way you and her are. Take care, pretty boy. I hope the little mouse is okay."

The tiger demon slinks back into the cover of the pines. I can't help but laugh to myself. Even the perverted tiger demon cared about Aiya. I wish she knew how loved she was. Aiya can make a cruel heart kind. She has the ability to enchant those around her without trying. There are times when I think jealousy will drive me mad but I can't be angry with anyone for loving Aiya. I've seen men stop in their tracks as we walk by. She holds the world captive but does not know it.

Aiya is asleep when I get home. I start the fire and grill the fish. While I'm waiting for her dinner and hot water to be ready I crawl into bed with her. I feel her forehead. She's not as warm as she was last night. Unable to resist, I touch all the stars on her body. Aiya is the one who seeks me out but things are different and I am the one waiting for her. Her hurt, is my hurt, and I scold myself for my selfishness.

My palm rests where her navel is and I feel the slight stirring inside her. To think we almost lost our child crushes me and I push the thought out of my mind. I scoot down and put my ear to the stars on her stomach and listen to my baby's heartbeat for the first time. It's very fast but faint. Aiya's heart echoes in the background, it is slow but steady.

"Aiya, you need to wake up." I whisper as I gently shake her shoulder. She is groggy but she opens her bleary eyes.

"Is something wrong?" she asks.

"No, but you need to eat. Here, Lady Kiyori wants you to drink this." She is fatigued but is able to sit up. I hand her the tea and a fish.

She seems weak and I sit next to her and let her lean on me while she sips the winterberry concoction and takes small bites.

"Thank you," she says.

"You don't have to thank me. I should have been doing this before."

"I like when you take care of me." She is too tired to smile but I can tell she wants to.

"I like it, too," I say. Maybe I am up for this challenge after all.

****

I told Aiya she shouldn't be dancing in the snow or jumping from the trees and to my surprise she agreed. Aiya tends to do as I say. Her faith in me is awe inspiring. I am trying to be the person she thinks I am. Now that she is feeling better she's been spending a lot of time with her friends. They are all excited for us.

"Are you going to join me?" she asks.

"No, I have some things to take care of."

"Like what?"

"It's a surprise," I say and kiss her. This makes her laugh.

"Okay. You're always welcomed." She slips out the door. I watch her enter Chiyo's house. Then I leave.

I've been using the times Aiya is with her friends as an opportunity to do jobs for the neighboring villages in exchange for human money. I protect men as they transport their goods and take care of demons plaguing farms. The people are generous. I don't mind spending my time being more helpful. The only problem is no one in Aiya's village will take my money. They say I can have everything for free. It bothers me.

"Brother Minoru told us about the boar demons that you slayed. You never have to pay for anything here, Riku," says the man at the apothecary.

"Are you sure?" I ask.

"Of course. You protect as though we are your pack. Thank you." His words are kind but they make my heart bleed into my stomach.

"Thank you."

I exit the shop with the items Lady Kiyori prescribed for Aiya. The next stop is the seamstress shop. In the neighboring village I bought a pattern of yellow and white silk I wanted for Aiya's present. The obi is red but not just any red, it's spider lily scarlet.

"I hope you like it, Riku. I wanted it to be perfect for her," says the seamstress. I hold out the money to her and she pushes it back into my hands, "No, I want you to have it. Please, it would bring me joy to give you two a gift." Her tree bark eyes are soft and sincere.

"If you insist," I say.

"I do. It's my pleasure."

"Thank you." I am genuinely grateful but vexed over my treatment. I wince as I enter Hajime's shop. This is a necessary evil. I try to hide my irritation.

"Riku, nice to see you. What brings you in?" asks Hajime. His clear voice twists a dagger between my eyes.

"It's my sword. I need it sharpened. There are a few nicks in the blade I would like repaired as well."

Hajime holds out his hands to it but I walk past him into the room where the weapons of Aiya's village are made. I set it down on the table for him.

"You won't be able to pick it up by yourself. At least three of you will be necessary to maintain the blade," I inform him. He looks at my sword with great interest.

"This blade is incredible. Where was it made?" he asks. His violet eyes shimmer as he admires the weapon of my people.

"In the volcano. It was crafted by fire demons with hellfire. That's why it didn't work on Kasai," I admit.

"I've never seen anything like this. It will take me three days. I will have my brothers help me."

"Thank you, Hajime." I hold out the money to him.

"No, no. I would never take your money, Riku."

"Why?" My question makes him laugh.

"I know you don't like me. I understand. Perhaps one day we can be friends. We both love Aiya, we have that in common. You saved our village and in more ways than one you saved her. I owe you everything." His answer makes me flinch. I hope he doesn't notice.

"What do you mean?" I ask.

"I've always wanted Aiya to be happy and now she is," he says.

My face is scorching hot.

"I have to go," I say and exit the shop with my head down. Why is it that I can obey without fail and fight wars but I can't handle the kindness of humans?

I wait for Aiya to get home and enjoy my time to myself. I crave her, but there are days where I want to lay in her bed and smell the scent of honey but be alone. My feelings are mixed and confusing most of the time since being with Aiya.

I must have fallen asleep because I wake up to Aiya's arms wrapped around me. Her hair is so long it covers her like a blanket. The image makes me smile and I feel so happy until I kiss her. Her face is hot again, like the morning I thought we'd lost our baby. She's asleep. I don't want to but I shake her awake.

"What is it, Riku?"

"You're burning up. Do you feel okay?" I ask.

"I've been having bad dreams."

"About what?"

"About him." She doesn't say his name but I know who she means.

"What happens in them?"

"I don't want to talk about it."

"Aiya, please. Tell me," I say too aggressively.

"No."

Aiya never says no to me. It used to bother me but right now I need her to tell me.

"Please, I'm begging you. I'm right here, Aiya. Please, tell me," I say. She sits up and I see her chest is flushed as is her face. It's like the stars are disappearing.

"I dream about Kasai being my baby's father. It disgusts me, Riku. I wake up in the middle of the night and want to die thinking about it," she says. Aiya's confession rips my soul apart.

"But you know it's not true. He's gone, you defeated him. It's just us now." I try to comfort her but feel like I am failing again.

"I know. They scare me though. They scare me more than anything."

I get out of bed and Aiya watches me as I fish around in my cloak. I pull out the items from the apothecary. I put a few drops of the medicinal oil into a cup of water for her.

"I was told this helps with fevers." I hand it to her and she looks up at me with wide eyes, "What?" I ask.

"Nothing," she smiles.

"Please, tell me." I don't like when we play this game.

"I just like seeing you like this," she says.

"Like what?" I ask.

"Fatherly. You seem happy."

"I am happy." I get back into bed with her and I fall asleep listening to two heartbeats in one.

CHAPTER SEVEN

Hurt is the Color Purple

"Let me go!" she yells.

"You said you wouldn't do this anymore, Aiya!" I shout.

"I want to have fun. You never let me have fun anymore." Aiya is trying to break my grasp and jump into the cedars touching the sky.

"Please, stop. I don't want you to hurt yourself."

The last three days have been difficult. Something has changed in Aiya. She doesn't want to listen to me. We fight like cats and dogs. I beg her all the time to just walk with me but she wants to run at breakneck speed.

"Let me go!" She keeps pulling but I keep my fist tight around her slender wrists.

"Why are you doing this to me?" I kneel down to see her better.

"I was going to ask you the same question," she hisses at me. It reminds me of Rena. A chill runs through me.

"What?" I ask.

"First you don't come back. Then you get to control everything I do! What gives you the right?" She hurls the words at me. This time it reminds me of Yuri.

"Aiya, I'm sorry. I–"

"You're always sorry!" Her shouting at me causes me to lose focus and I loosen my grasp. She runs off wearing the kimono I had made for her. She loved it a couple days ago. I worry what she may think about the gift now.

"Aiya! Come back here!"

I run after her. She is nowhere to be seen. She has done this to me many times but this time I know she isn't going to jump on me and kiss me.

"Dammit, Aiya. This isn't funny!"

I never yell at her. Not even during the times I want to. I let her scream at me the past few days. I can't raise my voice to her. I'm darting through the trees. The powdery white snow lifts in my wake and coats the low hanging branches.

"Aiya!" I call her name over and over again. I spend the entire day searching for her. There is no scent of honey or splash of summer in the winter. Where is she? Evening is here and she is nowhere to be seen. I go back into the village and knock on Chiyo's door.

"Hi Riku!" She can see the panic on my face and her tone changes. "What's wrong? Are you okay?"

"It's Aiya. She ran off on me. I can't find her. I've looked for her all day," I confess. Chiyo's eyes are stormy seas.

"I'm sorry. I haven't seen her."

"Thanks, Chiyo." I think she wants to say more but I am already gone. I go to Lady Kiyori's house.

"Riku?" What's going on?" The priestess asks with a worried tone.

"Aiya...ran off on me." I can't get the words out. The priestess and I communicate with our eyes and she grabs her sword.

"I will get Brother Minoru and the priestesses. We will search for her as well."

"Thank you," I say. The words are shards of metal in my throat. I go to the last place I want to but I do it because I need Aiya to be safe.

"Riku? What are you doing here?" Hajime's eyebrows are high on his forehead. I can see his brothers behind him staring at me.

"It's Aiya." I can barely speak.

"What's wrong?" he asks.

"She ran off on me this morning. I can't find her–" I haven't finished my sentence but the men grab their weapons and rush out of the house.

"We will help you look for her," says Hajime. His brothers nod to agree.

"Thank you. For everything, Hajime." My words seem to touch him because his face softens.

"I would do anything for Aiya so I would do anything for you." He smiles that thoughtful grin before he and his brothers run into the forest.

We look all night for her. I see hundreds of footprints in the snow from everyone searching. I've never been so worried. I find a place where I am sure no one is and lean against an oak tree while I vomit. I should have taken better care of her in the beginning. Why didn't I help her more? I wish she would have just told me what to do. I can take orders but I am at a loss as to what to do or say on my own.

Wolf demons pride themselves on being strong but I realize we are not strong at all. It is all a facade. I go back to Aiya's house hoping she'd be there but she's not. I sleep on her side of the bed and wonder why the gods would let this happen to me. Why would they let this happen to her?

"Riku?" It's Chiyo. I wake up alert and the embers of my heart turn into a roaring fire.

"What is it?"

"Come with me," she says. On my feet in an instant I run with her to the entrance of the village. Hajime, Natsume, and Daina are standing shoulder to shoulder.

"What's going on?" I don't mean to but I am tense and bark at her. She acts like it didn't happen.

"You have to see it," she says. Her sweet and pretty face is serious. I get up to where everyone is and stand next to Hajime. Looking up the hill where Kasai changed Aiya I see what is causing all the commotion. The tiger demon has Aiya in his arms. He isn't smirking or laughing as he walks with her down the hill. He nears and I see blood dripping between Aiya's legs. I lose control of my temper. I rush at him with a low growl in my throat.

"What did you do to her?" I snarl.

"I know this looks bad but I didn't do anything to her, I swear. Smell her." He hands her to me. He is telling the truth. I look down and see his arms are covered in her blood. Her face is peaceful.

"What happened?" I ask. His bare chest is also covered in the crimson liquid.

"She was running like a lunatic through the forest last night. I saw the monkey demons following her. They were saying things even I found repulsive. I didn't want anything bad to happen to the little mouse so I kept my eyes on her. She used her fire to elude them. But then I could smell blood. It was leaving a trail in the snow," he says.

"She allowed you to carry her?" The tiger demon looks away and I feel the blood turning into black tar in my heart.

"Don't be mad but I stole her breath. It's a cat demon thing. I didn't hurt her. I only wanted her to stop thrashing so I could bring her back to you. She'll wake up in a few hours. I'm sure she'll say I was quite noble," he laughs with his familiar wildcat trill.

"You wanted to bring her back to me. Why?"

"I told you, pretty boy. You and her are special. Take care," he says and with that the tiger demon retreats back into the forest.

***

Aiya has stopped bleeding but hasn't woken up yet. Lady Kiyori is trying her best to comfort me but it is useless. Brother Minoru is praying over Aiya. He unclasps his hands and places them on the stars below her navel. I see his brows furrow. Already tense I get up and pace the small room.

"Riku, can we step outside for a moment?" asks Lady Kiyori. I don't want to leave Aiya but I nod and embrace the falling snow with the priestess.

"What is it, Lady Kiyori?" I ask.

"I need to know a few things."

"What do you want to know?" My question makes the priestess take a deep breath and swallow.

"Has Aiya said anything to you about seeing Kasai?" The fire demon's name brings up bile to the back of my throat.

"She said she has dreams that he is her baby's father," I say. As the words leave my mouth I want to lean against a tree and vomit. The priestess conceals her shock.

"Any other strange or unusual behavior?"

"Aiya usually does what I say. She follows me everywhere I go. We spend most of our time happily together. The last few days she's been screaming at me nonstop. No matter what I do she is shouting at me and trying to run off. Everything I do is for her but she yelled at me for controlling her."

The priestess looks at me again.

"Riku, I think it is best if Brother Minoru explains something to you." She gestures for us to return into the house. The monk is praying over Aiya again. He has incense lit and his eyes are closed. "Brother Minoru?" The priestess interrupts him.

He doesn't seem to mind and looks at both of us, the creases of his smile gone from his face.

"Riku, please come sit with me," says the monk. He beckons for me to come closer.

"What is it?"

"What do you know about fire demons?" he asks.

"Nothing really. They make our people's weapons with hellfire," I say. The monk takes off his necklace and wraps it around his wrist. He places it on Aiya's stomach and his bright eyes turn cloudy.

"When a fire demon makes a deal with someone they take a drop of blood from that person back to The Underworld. They use it to create a Wraith. That is what they use to invade dreams, manipulate thoughts, and influence decisions," says Brother Minoru.

"What is a Wraith?" I ask.

"It is the ghost of the soul. Aiya still has her heart and her soul but something is very wrong, Riku."

"What's happening to her?"

"The darkness...it's growing in her heart. It's suffocating the baby," he says.

The monk's eyes are wet. For some reason I look over to the priestess to comfort me. She gives me a remorseful nod and places her hand on my shoulder.

"What do I do to save her?" I ask. The monk and the priestess exchange a knowing glance.

"You're going to have to go down into The Underworld to get her Wraith. Until it's returned to her the darkness will continue to ravage her body. Aiya won't be the same anymore," he says. The monk's words have me on my feet and ready to go.

"How do I get there?" I ask. The priestess stands up but the monk remains with his hand over Aiya's starry skin.

"I'm sorry, Riku. But Brother Minoru and I aren't strong enough to open the portal to The Underworld. You will need someone of enormous spiritual power. I wish we could help you as you have helped us," says Lady Kiyori. The priestess covers her heart and bows to me.

"I know someone with that kind of power," I say. This shocks them both.

"Who?" They ask at the same time.

"My sister, Yama. She was our people's spiritual leader. Over a decade ago she told me I would carry something precious in my cloak through sacred grounds. I was led by the white deer, the gods' messenger, to Aiya's village all those years ago." Lady Kiyori and Brother Minoru look at Aiya and then me.

"You two were destined to be together." Lady Kiyori whispers the words and chokes on them.

"Can you watch over Aiya for me, please? I will be back in three days," I say.

"Of course. We would do anything for you and Aiya," says the monk. The tears stain his blue robe purple and indigo.

"Thank you," I say and I run as fast as I can towards the mountains I swore I'd never go near again.

***

Never taking a break I sprint through the forest day and night. I can't sleep. I can't eat. There is nothing more important to me than Aiya. How could I be so careless with something so precious? The gods gave me a beautiful gift. I am a man with broken sight. I was blind.

I'm nearing the first village I ever saw. The one where I met Kasai. There isn't any time to waste but my curiosity forces me to take a glance into the place where I first fell in love with humanity. It appears the village is doing better. The fields are full of rice and root vegetables. There are more shops and houses. The wind picks up and I smell the scent of a wolf. Not just any wolf though, it's my sister Yuri.

I exit the treeline and enter the village. The people stare at me but don't seem frightened. I follow the scent until I see long white hair. She's facing away from me standing next to a man. He puts his arm around her. This must be the boy my sister fell in love with.

"Yuri?" I call her name and she turns around. I'm shocked by what I see. My sister is swollen with pregnancy. The man she is with smiles a grin so pure it could make even my warmonger father cry. I can see why Yuri fell in love with him.

"Riku!" My sister runs towards me with intense speed and embraces me. She looks up and I see her eyes are no longer puffy and sad. Even all grown up she only comes up to my chest. She looks just like our mother but more beautiful.

"Yuri, I can't believe it." I eye her stomach that's ready to burst. "You're pregnant." I whisper the last part. I think of the half demon I saw. The family in the forest.

"This is my husband, Toshio. He is the boy I told you I loved a long time ago. I couldn't take living in the mountains anymore," she starts. I have no words and stare at her. Thankfully she keeps speaking. "I protect the village from the demons that differ from you and I. I'm so happy to see you, big brother. Our hearts are the same," says my sister.

Yuri squeezes my arms. She looks me up and down. Her husband joins us and stands by her side.

"I'm so glad to meet you, Riku. You inspired Yuri to leave home. I have loved her for a long time. I thought we'd never be together. Thank you," says my sister's husband. He has shoulder length brown hair and jade eyes. There is something alluring about him. I nod but I'm speechless.

"What are you doing here?" she asks. My sister's cool gray eyes see all. She knows something is wrong.

"I am going back home. I need Yama," I say.

"What? No! You can't, Riku!" Yuri takes my hands in hers. "Ryo has destroyed our once enviable kingdom. They live in ruins. Rena transformed and remains a beast. Ryo keeps her chained up at the base of the mountain to deter our enemies which have grown in number. Hoshi can't keep the people's faith. Everything is in shambles, big brother."

"I need Yama. The woman I love is being tortured by a fire demon." Yuri covers her mouth and sheds a tear. Her husband holds her waist to comfort her. "Yuri, what do you know about fire demons?" I ask.

"They are from The Underworld and their power is unlike any other. The ability to invade dreams and cross over from the spectral plain to our earthly ground. They feed on fear, weakness, and greed. Fire demons are keepers of the darkness. When we succumb to our demonic rage it is they who we lose ourselves to," she cries. I clench my fist and grit my teeth.

"I will do anything for her. I don't care if I die down there. Life isn't worth living without her," I say with a tight jaw. Toshio puts his hands on my sister's shoulders and pulls her close to him.

"Then you must go. If it is for love it is always worth it. There is nothing more precious than the one we love," says the man with jade eyes. They see right through me. He lets my sister go and she embraces me again.

"Be careful, big brother. I love you," she says.

"I love you, too." I take one last look at my pregnant sister and her husband. With a heavy heart I take off towards the castle.

***

Rena is chained but pulls at her restraints, her black blood spilling out as she jerks her massive body. My big sister has succumbed to the darkness. This makes my heart pound in my ears. I can't let anything bad happen to Aiya. Seeing my eldest sister in such a sad state upsets me more than I thought it would. I hated her but I don't want to see her like this.

She roars at me and attempts to charge but can't reach me. Her chain doesn't allow her to go too far. Her paws dig up the dirt and knock over the cedars. The boulders roll down the mountain as she paces. It's obvious she is bored and irritated. Her eyes are rose red. She looks at me like she remembers me for a moment but goes back to howling and pulling at her chain.

As I near the castle I see our kingdom is falling apart. The arena is deteriorating. It used to be spotless white marble and steel. The walls are cracked and there are blood stains on the dirt inside. The fields are barren. It looks like the crops haven't been growing for quite some time. Our garden is full of dead flowers. They have turned black and brown. The courtyard is littered with excrement. How could Ryo let our home become so foul?

I see what's causing the disgusting mess in the yard. Half a dozen raccoon demons scurry past me. The creatures vary in size. One is small like an ordinary raccoon but he has red eyes and wears blue trousers. The others are tall but not quite as tall as me. They have belts holding throwing daggers and pouches of unknown powder. The demons reek of excrement and decomposing flesh. It's a horrible stench. The abhorrent scent causes my eyes to water.

I walk up to the castle and knock on the door three times. Waiting for what seems like forever it appears no one is going to answer. I almost fling the door open. I'm greeted by Hoshi. Her eyes go wide with disbelief.

"Riku?" Her voice is shrill and raw, not how I remember it being. She has dark circles under her juniper eyes. The sunlight hair isn't vibrant and shiny anymore. I should have known Ryo would do this to her. She chose to marry him and this encourages me to disregard her sadness.

"I need to talk to Yama," I say.

"Little brother, didn't I banish you?" Ryo is behind Hoshi with his hand on her shoulder. She grimaces as he speaks next to her ear.

"I just need to talk to Yama. Please," I say. This makes Ryo laugh, an arrogant chuckle. It makes me want to rip out his vocal cords.

"Get out of here you filthy stray. You're not welcomed home," he growls.

"Riku?" Yama shoves them both out of the way and puts her white silk hands on my face. I pull at her sleeve with relief. She looks the same as the day I left. Her red lips are in a tight line. The gold eyes we share are full of questions.

"Yama," I sigh. I am so happy to see my big sister.

"Little sister, why are you consorting with the worthless whelp?" Ryo keeps his hands on Hoshi. She looks like she would rather die.

"Don't even, big brother. Your wife can't keep our people's faith. I am the one who whispers in their ears and makes them believe. I think it is you who is the worthless one," she says. Yama's words flow in and out of the king's ears and he turns bright crimson.

"That is it! Get out of here! I won't have another filthy stray in this family," shouts Ryo.

"Fine with me. There is nothing sacred or beautiful about this place anymore. Enjoy your wasteland. I can't believe you let the tanuki demon in," says Yama. She takes my arm and we walk the path down the mountain. We don't talk until we pass Rena at the bottom. Yama doesn't even glance at her.

"Yama, what happened?" I ask.

"What we knew would happen. Ryo keeps poor company. He let the tanuki demon and his band of racoons in. Ryo wanted Hoshi to have too many children too fast and her body couldn't handle it. He needed more soldiers so he made an arrangement with the tanuki. He is a shapeshifter and a good liar. Ryo can't see what is right in front of him."

"And what is that?"

"That he is no longer the true king. The tanuki demon leads the wars. He has introduced the faith of his people and it contradicts ours. It has caused many conflicts in regards to our spiritual teachings," she says.

"What happened to Yahei?" I ask. I don't want to know the answer.

"Yahei is second in command next to the tanuki. He is just as ruthless as our father but not an independent thinker. He follows Ryo as though is a god."

I stop walking. I can't process what has happened to my home, to my family. Yama lifts up my chin to get a better look at me.

"I missed you, big sister." I smile at her but it hurts.

"I missed you, too. Now tell me, why did you come to talk to me?" she asks.

"The woman I love is being tortured by a fire demon. I have to go to The Underworld to get her Wraith back. I need your help," I say.

"Take me to her," says my sister and I pick up the pace.

***

As we approach the village it starts to snow again. The snowflakes stick in my eyelashes. I can barely feel them though. I am numb. My sister tries to comfort me but she lets me sulk. As Yama and I walk through the village they stop and stare. My sister is taller than all of them, almost as tall as me. Her white and red kimono drags on the ground.

She is a ghost with bright red lips and gold eyes. The villagers bow to us as we pass. My sister is polite and bows back. I hear Aiya scream and run towards Lady Kiyori's house. My sister is fast and stays by my side.

"Let me go. Stop! You're hurting me!"

It's Aiya. I'm outside the priestess's home. I almost rip the door off. The scene in front of me confuses and horrifies me. Aiya is tied up, her wrists are restrained by some kind of silky rope. There are bruises on her arms. She is baring her canines and screaming at Brother Minoru. The monk is trying to get her to eat.

"What are you doing to her?" I bark. The monk and priestess stare at me. They have never appeared frightened of me but they do now. My sister stands at my side and puts her hand on my shoulder.

"Riku, please come with me." The priestess ushers us outside.

"What are you doing to her? I thought you said you would take care of her?" I growl at Lady Kiyori. I know I shouldn't but I can't help it.

"You have to know we love Aiya, we would never do anything to hurt her. She did something, Riku. I am at a loss for words," she says.

"What did she do?" I ask.

"She...tried to cut the baby out. Brother Minoru stopped her in time but she has a deep gash across her stomach. She refuses to eat. Her constant thrashing keeps opening the wound. I'm sorry, Riku. I tried my best. I have failed you," says the priestess.

She bows to me and my sister. Lady Kiyori is on her knees. Yama puts her arms around me and I hang my head.

"Is the baby okay?" I ask.

"For now. But the darkness is taking over," says the priestess. I pull away from my sister and push past Lady Kiyori. I kneel down next to Aiya. She glares at me.

"You broke your promise," she hisses.

"What?"

"You said you would never leave me. You've been gone for three days. Look at me, Riku! Look at what they're doing to me!"

Aiya flails and her kimono opens revealing a large square bandage. Red ink seeps out of the bottom. Brother Minoru is trying to hold her down but she is fighting him.

"Please, Aiya. I am only trying to help you," says the monk. She spits in his face. He wipes it away with the sleeve of his robe. It doesn't matter though, he continues to try and calm her.

"I didn't leave you. I went to get you help. Please, Aiya. Please, come back to me." My voice is a shaky rasp. The love of my life, the light in the darkness, my summer in winter glares at me with hatred.

"Your sad puppy dog eyes make me sick. Just get away from me!" Hearing such horrible words in her beautiful voice breaks my heart and hot salty water spills out.

"Aiya…" I whisper her name to call her back.

"I don't want this thing inside me and I don't want you!"

She pulls her ring off with her teeth and spits it at my feet. The sound of gold hitting the wood floor is the echo of a bell. I pick it up with a trembling hand and step outside. The winter air freezes the tears on my face. Brother Minoru follows me out and takes my hand with the ring in it in both of his.

"She doesn't mean it, Riku. You know Aiya doesn't feel that way," says the monk.

"You heard her. She doesn't love me anymore," I say.

"You can't believe that. Someone down in The Underworld is making her say these things."

"What if this is how she really feels?" I ask. I feel the shape of the ring in my palm and the heat of Brother Minoru's hands on mine.

"Aiya believed in you when we all told her not to. Don't give up on her now."

The monk's words hit me in the gut with incredible force. I nod to let him know I'm listening but I can't talk anymore. My sister stands by me and the monk's eyes widen. They bow to each other.

"Can I meet her?" asks my sister.

The monk looks at me and I nod to give my permission. Yama steps inside and I can hear Aiya screaming again. It stops abruptly. My sister steps out with Aiya in her arms. She is unconscious. "I need you to take me to the nearest small body of water. A pond or a hot spring." I know exactly where to take her.

"Follow me," I say and we vanish into the gray-white.

We arrive at the hot spring where Aiya and I went sometimes. Aiya is wearing a white and pink kimono. It's not one of hers.

"Riku, do you trust me?" asks Yama.

"Yes." The word leave my lips and my sister shoves Aiya underneath the water. She holds her down and closes her gold eyes. I'm about to tear Aiya from her grasp but Yama freezes the hot spring.

"What did you do?" I never knew the extent of my sister's power.

"I can only hold her for three days. This will freeze her in time. The darkness won't be able to grow."

"Yama, I need you to open a portal to The Underworld."

"I can do that. But you're going to need help," she says.

"No, I can't ask anyone to go down there with me."

"But you will. I had a vision, little brother."

"What did you see?" I ask.

"You will not be able to remove Aiya from the depths of The Underworld. It will be a man with violet eyes and a pure heart. He will have the power to bring her back."

CHAPTER EIGHT

Guardian

I watch my sister try to explain to Hajime the depths of her spiritual power and the visions she had. He looks into her gold eyes and nods every so often.

"Yes, I see it now," says Yama.

"What do you see?" he asks.

"Why you will be the one to bring her back." My sister puts her hand to Hajime's broad chest.

"Why is that?" Hajime doesn't seem afraid of the challenge at all. He asks only out of curiosity.

"Your heart is the purest I have ever seen. Most people have a good heart that is touched by darkness from time to time. It isn't a bad thing, it just is. But your heart is different, Hajime. The darkness has never touched it. You have never felt envy, greed, or pride. I see it right here."

My sister pushes her palm into him. I know I have no right to be but I'm jealous. Why didn't Aiya just choose him instead?

"Riku, your sword will not work in The Underworld. Come with me," he says. Hajime leads us into his shop. He brings out a sword in a red leather sheath. A blessed weapon. "Aiya had me make this for you. It's special," he says.

I pull the sword from the leather to inspect it. Not half the size of mine but it's exquisite.

"What makes it special?" I ask.

"Aiya gave me a lock of her hair to throw in with the straw for ash. A piece of her is in that weapon. It is what I did to Aiya's knife, the one she defeated Kasai with."

"Thank you," I say.

"Follow me," says my sister.

She guides us through the forest in silence. We come upon a portion of grass where nothing has grown. No saplings or wild flowers. Not even a weed stuck out from under the snow. Yama motions for us to stop and walks into the middle.

She takes a dagger from her obi and slits her palm. My sister kneels with the bloody hand touching the ground while she whispers into the other. I have never known how it works or understood the greatness of spiritual strength.

The forest floor rumbles and snow falls from the canopy. Hajime looks at me and I nod at him. He has the same unreadable expression Aiya and the priestess have. My sister steps away from the blood soaked snow. It starts to melt and warp into a hole in the ground.

My sister tears bark from a nearby oak tree and slathers her scarlet palm all over the pieces. She begins throwing them into the hole in the ground and stairs are formed. The heat hits my face and sweat forms at my hairline. Yama uses the dagger to cut off a long lock of silvery white hair. She whispers something to it and ties it around my left wrist.

"What's this?" I ask.

"When you have Aiya's Wraith untie the knot. Whisper the words *'bring me to life'*

into the hair. It will be your way back." Yama caresses my face. I missed her so much.

"Thank you, Yama. For everything." I shock my sister with my embrace.

"I would do anything for you, little brother. Nothing without you," she says as she puts two fingers to her lips before pointing at me.

"Nothing without you," I mimic. Hajime is looking at us. I think our culture interests him.

"Hajime, are you ready?" I ask.

"Yes," he says.

"Let's go."

I glance over my shoulder to see Yama. Her wavy white hair and kimono catch the wind. The stairs to The Underworld go on for at least a thousand steps. Hajime is alert but not anxious. How can he be so brave?

"Riku." My name in his mouth forces me to swallow.

"What is it?" I turn around to see him staring at me.

"Your sister said she had a vision of you saving Aiya. That you were destined to meet. Is that true?" His question at this inappropriate time irritates me but I answer.

"Yes. The gods' messenger, the white deer, brought me to Aiya all those years ago. I thought I was no one but I was chosen. I don't know why. All I do is fail her," I say. I didn't mean to say the last part out loud. Hajime holds my elbow with a fierce grip.

"Don't say that. You can't believe that," he says. His violet eyes aren't kind and predictable anymore.

"I can't even bring her back, Hajime. It has to be you. It was you who saved her from the fire demon the first time."

"If you didn't save her that day Kasai came from her I would have never met her. Please, Riku. Don't say you've failed. Aiya has never felt that way about you. You must have faith in yourself," he says. Hajime lets me go and we continue walking down the stairs going on for an eternity.

Once we reach the bottom the scent of decay and rot is potent. The walls heave and sigh like lungs with black tar stuck inside. Everything wheezes and creaks as we pass. There are black birds of various sizes with red eyes everywhere. My father told me the crow is a soul collector. It guides them to the place of their rest.

Hajime stares up at them as we pass and they caw at him. The sound is harsh in my ears. Almost as bad as the scent. We weave through dripping caverns and hallways that seem to go nowhere. The Underworld stretches on endlessly. I don't even know where to begin to look for Aiya's Wraith. The twinge in my chest returns and I pick up the pace. I need her. I can't live without her.

"Riku–" Hajime grabs my shoulder.

"What?" I ask. He points down and I notice an array of different symbols on hexagon shaped platforms.

"I think we should be careful where we step," he says. I haven't been paying enough attention. I get the hint.

"You're right."

I'm more cautious as to not trigger whatever the emblems bring. There is scarlet mist swirling through the entirety of The Underworld. Blood is seeping out of the walls. There are eyeballs opening as we pass by. Their blinking makes a moist clapping noise in our wake. My spine aches. The red mist is thick but I can see someone in front of us.

"Hello?" I call. Nothing. "Show yourself!" I demand.

There is the familiar laughter of Kasai and the blood in my veins turns caustic. Everything comes to a halt.

"What do we have here? A stray," says a sonorous voice. A demon wearing a long red cloak and the skull of a vulture approaches. I am beyond myself when I see what is in his arms. It's Aiya's Wraith. She is nude and appears asleep. I draw my sword.

"Give her back!" I bark.

"Not so fast, lover boy." The demon removes the skull he wears and I see Kasai's face smirking at me.

"Kasai," I growl.

"Not quite. I'm his twin brother, Kaji."

"What are you doing to Aiya?" I am becoming enraged.

"Whatever I want," he says.

The fire demon sticks his serpent tongue in Aiya's mouth. The eyes of the Wraith glow red. She has no pupils and appears to be in a daze. I attempt to rush him but Hajime grabs my sleeve.

"Don't fall for it, Riku. He's baiting us," says Hajime. I want to rip his wrist off but I don't. I calm myself down.

"I can make her say whatever I want. How do you know all those times she said she loved you it wasn't me inside her?" Kaji's laughter is unrestrained and the flames of The Underworld grow around us. His scent is putrid, worse than Kasai's.

"Damn you," I roar.

"It's a shame. I was really looking forward to her being my sister-in-law. My brother even said we could take turns!" shouts Kaji.

The fire demon's hand begins roaming Aiya's body. He touches her in the places only I'm allowed to touch her. I feel my eyes glowing red with demonic hatred.

"Riku! No!" Hajime puts his rough hands around my face and looks into my core. "The fire demon wants you to lose control. Don't give into him. That's not Aiya. She is waiting for you up there," he says as he motions towards the ceiling of The Underworld. A thousand bats squeak with high pitched voices echoing off the pus filled walls. Everything sways, bloats, and exhales.

"Thank you," I say. I relax my shoulders and put the sword away.

"She doesn't have much time. The darkness inside her will take over. After she succumbs to it she will be my bride. The baby inside her will be mine as well," says Kaji who grins as he puts the vulture skull back over his face.

"No! I'll never let that happen!" I shout.

"You already have," says Kaji in his menacing voice that echoes off the walls. The serpent tongue slithers across his teeth. He licks Aiya's face before disappearing into the red fog. I want to collapse and disappear inside myself. Hajime takes my arm and pulls me into the mist. The walls constrict and expand. They are lined with humanoid creatures in chains.

They stand taller than I and are covered in scabs, crusted over with infection. Eyes bulge a bright blue. Their cheeks are hollow but their stomachs are engorged like they have swallowed a melon whole. The yellow and green pus oozes out as they struggle, opening their tiny wounds over and over. Reeking of rotting flesh and bile they groan, tinging the air with their acrid breath. It makes me want to vomit but what Kaji was doing to Aiya's Wraith makes me want to vomit more.

"Don't listen to him. You can't believe anything he says."

I nod to let Hajime know I'm listening but I feel like dying.

***

I can tell Hajime is tired but he won't say so. There is no way to tell time down here. It is night time dark and red at all hours.

"We should take a break," I suggest.

"No, I'm fine," he says, as I knew he would.

"I insist." I stand but lean against the ruby brick wall of The Underworld's halls.

"Okay."

Hajime sits down and runs his hands through his dark hair. We rest in silence. The caw of the crows flying over us combined with the eternal hellfire blazing is deafening. I can hear the pus and blood oozing out of the cracks in the walls. The caves have a thousand red eyes looking at us from the shadows. Geysers reeking of toxicity release red steam into the air periodically. It's so abhorrent my nose bleeds and I taste it in the back of my throat.

We continue wandering into the depths of this hellish place. I keep glancing over my shoulder to check on Hajime. There is an opening up ahead and in front of us is a giant maze. The thick scarlet fog makes it difficult to see the twists and turns. It won't be easy to spy the demons I know lurk within.

"Hajime, stay close to me," I say.

He nods his head and we wade into the mist. It seems to go on and on. I worry we will never make it back to Aiya in time. How could I let this happen? If I am successful I vow to put her first. I will stay by her side, every night, every day, until she tells me to go. She is my precious gift from the gods and I will cherish her.

"Riku." Hajime says my name. I turn around to see him looking down one of the tunnels of the maze.

"What?" I ask.

"Listen," he says.

Hajime and I look to the ground. There is a sickly slithering noise. Followed by hissing. It sounds venomous and the dark energy around us increases. I stand next to Hajime, feeling protective. There is no way I can fail him and Aiya. If that happens I may just stay down here where I belong.

The scent changes and I smell a reptile. It's tinged with the burning rot of The Underworld's black blood. The mist swirls around us. Hajime holds himself well. I draw the weapon Aiya had made for me. May her love be my salvation. I look to my left and see the cause of the scent. It's a massive snake demon, as large as the centipede that wrapped around Aiya's village. I grab Hajime's arm and we run.

The creature slinks through the maze. It knows every entrance and exit. There is no way it will let us pass. I will have to kill it but I need to make sure Hajime is safe. We weave through the twist and maneuver to avoid the snake. It flicks its tongue and tastes our fear in the air. The red eyes glow with demonic rage and it roars. Thankfully I find a place to hide Hajime. There's a crack in the wall. It's just big enough for one person.

"Hajime, wait here for me."

"No, I should go with you," he says.

"Please, I need you to be safe. Wait here," I say a bit too aggressively. He nods and steps

into the safety of the dark. "Thank you," I say and take off in search of the serpent.

I press my back against the moist walls and peek around corners. The energy is poisonous. It won't be easy to kill a creature this evil, this massive, but I will do what I have to. I need to save Aiya. She is my everything. I think about the last time she kissed me. How happy she looked. I shake away the beautiful memory and focus.

The snake finds me and lunges. It misses, the skull hits the wall but it is incredibly strong and appears to feel no pain. It roars again as it strikes the bricks, smashing the wall into pieces. Red and black dust is everywhere. It's hard to see. Then I notice it. The sword is glowing. Why is it glowing? Hajime said Aiya put herself in this weapon. I was remembering her kiss. It will be her love saving me a thousand times over. The more I think about how much I love her the greater the glow of the weapon.

"Come at me!" I demand the serpent to strike.

It follows my command and I shove the sword down its throat. I pull up and slash through its brains. The rotten blood sprays everywhere but it continues to fight me. Its fangs drip clear liquid that dissolves the red rocks lining the maze.

I elude the creature and lure it away from where I hid Hajime. To my horror another serpent appears. It's a quarter of the size of the other. This one is different, it has spikes on its back. It lifts up its body and screeches. I see it also has eight legs. The walking serpent charges at me and I block it with the blessed weapon.

It lunges repeatedly. I manage to dodge it but I can't land a hit. The larger snake demon is behind me, I can feel the energy shift. The smaller beast rushes past me. Turning around I see two more snake demons. One has emerald eyes and dagger-like horns. The other is white with all black eyes. Its tongue is blue and the venomous scent it emits is corrosive. The four of them stare me down with soulless gazes. My strength relies on her love.

Remember Aiya's hand on my chest, her sleeping in my arms, and the beautiful voice in which she sang about me, I charge through the demons and start slashing.

They hiss and drip poison. Their tongues are slimy and are decorated with pus filled blisters. Their own venom destroys them from the inside. I slide through the red dust and chop them into pieces. Hacking away at their bodies causes the diseased blood to shower all over me but I continue. I smell it burn my hair and feel it eating away at the skin on my cheek. My ears sizzle and itch from the toxic liquid.

With the power of the blessed sword and the memory of her voice I am able to slay the serpents. The walking snake is the fastest and it darts back and forth. It aims to strike my heart but my armor blocks it. Slicing off its hideous spindly legs meant for a spider it falls over and squirms. It screeches as it evaporates.

The stench is so foul my eyes water. Black blood tints the red dust. I cut the horned snake's head off and blue blood reeking of festering rot pours out. It floods the maze and I jump up and over the walls to avoid it. I return to where Hajime is hiding.

"You can come out now," I say.

"Riku, you're covered in blood! Are you okay?" asks Hajime.

"I'm fine. Don't worry about me. We should continue." I start walking without waiting for his answer. I know he will follow me.

"That was impressive," says the fire demon.

"Kaji."

I look up to see him sitting on a throne. It's gold and lined with red and blue jewels. The fire demon's wrists are adorned with bracelets made of silver and the skulls of tiny animals. Aiya's Wraith lies in his lap. His hand is in between her legs. I bite my tongue until metallic fluid coats my canines.

"What? Do you not like it when I touch her?" he asks. Kaji lifts up the vulture skull with his free hand. He blows a kiss at me and sticks out his disgusting tongue.

"Why are you doing this to her?" I shout.

"A deal is a deal. You know she found him attractive, don't you?

I saw it in her dreams. She is afraid of him but she finds my face handsome," he says. The fire demon embraces Aiya's Wraith and I am about to lose it.

"Riku, don't." Hajime bores into me with his violet eyes.

Kaji vanishes into the fog. I want to chase after him but everything is an illusion down here. Hajime needs me to keep him safe and running off on him is the worst thing I could do. I put my head down and keep walking.

"Aiya should have married you," I announce. Hajime stops walking. I can't bear to turn around.

"No, Riku. She loves you," he says.

"But why? I haven't been much help to her."

"That's not how love works."

"How does it work then?" I spit.

"I don't know how it works myself," he smiles to himself. "I proposed to Chiyo last month." My jaw drops.

"What?" I ask.

"She said 'yes'. We were going to tell you two but then Aiya got sick. It didn't seem appropriate."

"But you're still in love with Aiya..." Hajime laughs at my words.

"I will always love her. But I am in love with Chiyo. She has captured my heart. We plan on getting married and having children soon," he says.

"Congratulations." I'm sincere but it hurts me more than I thought it would.

"Thank you," he says. Our boots echo in the red abyss.

***

It storms periodically in The Underworld. The atmosphere is hot, humid, and red steam is emitted from the geysers littering the crimson sand. There are massive shadow monsters, they groan and creak as they trudge through the dunes. They are dull and do not notice us. Smaller creatures resembling rabbits with horns and red eyes scurry through the empty plain. They hide in the hills.

"You know she likes it down here. She enjoys being my slave," says Kaji.

He approaches from the left. Aiya's Wraith lies sleeping in his wicked grasp. Her arm hangs loosely and I wish to prop it up. I want to be with Aiya right now. How could I have ever taken her for granted? I'll die down here before I let her go.

"You're lying!" I snarl.

My eyes are heating up in my skull. The darkness is taking hold of me. Hajime grabs me by the collar.

"Don't. He wants you to succumb to the rage. If you do, he wins. He is the darkness, Riku. Please, don't give in. He'll have Aiya forever," says Hajime. His grip is a solid fist against my skin. I shake away the rage.

"She thinks you left her. You kind of did. What kind of husband and father does that?" asks Kaji. The fire demon cackles and small fires build around his boots.

"I would never leave her!" I shout.

"I know everything about her. I see inside her soul, lover boy. She longs for you, she loves you so much it aches, yet you deny her. I see how she waits for you. When I am inside her I feel her pain. It tastes like cinnamon. She would wait for you forever if I let her. It's only a matter of time though. She's becoming fond of me. She sees that I am the better man!" Kaji smirks as he talks.

"Stop lying. She would never love you."

The anger in me is ugly, vile, and merciless. On impulse I think of murdering Kaji. I know it's what he wants.

"Why do you seek to take something that isn't yours, Riku?" Kaji's tongue rolls out of his mouth and tastes the Wraith's starry skin.

The hair on the back of my neck rises and I think about biting off his hand, then eating his tongue for dinner. Hajime looks at me with those violet eyes that tell no lies and I hang my head in shame.

"She's not yours. She's mine. She's always been mine," I growl. It's rough in my throat. The tone is low and animalistic. I don't dare look up to see what he's doing to Aiya.

"Is that so? Prove it," says Kaji and he dissipates into the air. I fall to my knees and clench my fist. I grit my teeth and stifle my vomit. The rage threatens to overtake me but I fight it. I have to fight it.

"Riku, are you okay?" asks Hajime. He puts his hand on my shoulder and I knock him away.

"No!" I bark. Hajime doesn't look offended. Instead he sits down next to me. He doesn't say anything and we watch ghastly beasts take painful steps until the guilt consumes me. "I'm sorry," I apologize. It's the right thing to do. He is trying to help me.

"It's fine. I understand. Kaji is afraid we will win. That's why he keeps egging you on. I sense he can't keep the Wraith with him. He must leave The Underworld from time to time," he says. Hajime's voice is wise and calm.

"How do you have faith?"

The question has no answer but I ask it anyway. Hajime sits with it for quite some time. A gray and black cloud passes over us and ruby raindrops hit the sand. They coat our clothes and leave a sleek residue in our hair. There is no shelter here. We let the unholy water bleed over us. The scent is pungent and metallic. The mix of steel, copper, and silver gags me. I swallow but it's unsatisfying.

"I just do," is all he says. The expression he wears is continuously charming. It irritates me but I chide myself on my ungratefulness. Hajime is the one who saved Aiya and he will save her again.

"Let's go," I say and help him up.

We tread through the sandy terrain. The wind is fierce and the scarlet sand is shards of glass in my eyes. I look back to see Hajime struggling to see. Flying creatures resembling lizards and frogs cast large shadows on the red sand. They do not bother us but I keep my eye on them. I am used to blizzards and harsh rains. Hajime is confused by my sudden stop but I take off my cloak and wrap it around him. The gales down here are unforgiving but it helps.

"Thank you." His violet eyes are wide with surprise.

"You're welcome."

CHAPTER NINE

The Darkest Place

The Underworld reeks of sulfuric rot. It makes me wince as I inhale its abhorrent stench. The inside of my nose is blistered and bloody from breathing in the polluted air. Hajime keeps coughing. The scent must affect him as well. We've exited the red desert and enter the chaotic mess. This part of The Underworld is without wind, without rain, but the dunes lining the crimson ravine are filled with decaying corpses, cloth, and metal. It's piled high with rubbish in this part. A wasteland with no end in sight.

There are tiny demons with red eyes skittering across the hills but they don't pay mind to us. They appear to be lizards but I'm not sure what they are. I watch as they consume the dead flesh and broken shards of steel. Disturbed scavengers indeed. The lizard demons make chirping and hissing noises. The sound causes my skin to crawl.

The sky above us is blood red. Two black suns pass each other but do not set. There are no stars and this depresses me more than it should. Everything about this place is depressing. I don't understand how time or weather works down here. Hajime and I keep trudging forward in search of the Wraith.

"The wolf was once lonely," sings Kaji.

Damn him. That was Aiya's song for me. I hate the idea of him roaming around in her head and looking into our private moments. He stands at a distance but I can see him squeezing Aiya's breast. The demonic hatred is spoiling my blood and I feel it bubble with rage.

"Don't you dare!" I bark. This makes Kaji laugh. The vulture skull is covering his face. His chest heaves and sighs with amusement.

"Turn back now, Riku. You're wasting your time," says Kaji.

"I'll never stop looking for her." I grit my teeth as I say the words.

"You might find her but you'll never be able to take her from me."

Kaji removes the vulture skull to show me his hideous grin full of teeth. It gives him pleasure to taunt me like this. Hajime grabs my shoulder the way a brother would.

"Don't listen to him, Riku. You can't trust the fire demon. Look at him. He is a false king. Sitting on his throne in his wasteland with a ghost on his lap. Not only does he envy you but he is afraid," says Hajime without removing his gaze from Kaji whose eyes go wide with surprise. I've never seen Kasai or Kaji look surprised.

"Well, isn't this delightful? A man who loved Aiya and the man who would die for her working together," says Kaji as he fades into the red mist.

I spit up the blood I've been holding in my mouth. I bit the inside of my cheek raw. Bits of flesh hang in my mouth and I taste myself.

"Thanks," I mutter.

Hajime keeps walking and I follow. I wish to say more but I can't find the words. The energy shifts and pulls me out of my thoughts. "Hajime, do you feel that?" I ask.

He turns around but I see it first. A giant scorpion with a woman's face on its forehead. The creature is made out of the rubbish and makes grating noises as it animates its body. It lets out a roar even the gods would fear.

I rush past Hajime and jump. While in the air I come down and attempt to slice through the creature's massive claw made of metal and soiled body parts. It tosses me and I land on my back with the other claw coming down at me. Hajime grabs me and we watch the claw sink into the red dust where I just was.

The garbage beast charges at us. I try to be kind but I fling Hajime away from me into the pile of body parts. I need to keep him safe and alive. Aiya's Wraith–my sister said he will be the one to remove her from this hellish place. Her visions have been accurate.

I can't distinguish the metallic scent of blood from the silver and copper in the hills. Now we are closer to them I can better see the fabric. Kimonos stained purple and red. The monsters here eat people. Limbs and pelvic bones are their refuse. Lizards with lesions all over their bodies gnaw at the leftover tissue on the rib cages and sternums.

The ground is gummy from filth. It's stained brown and copper. I dodge the foul creature's immediate attack. Foamy brown liquid seeps out of the ground where the scorpion strikes. I manage to land a hit but it is relentless. Besides the face on it I can't think of any other weak point. The whole body is covered in a thick iron exoskeleton, limiting my ability to injure it. I could try and hack into bits but I don't have time to waste fighting this thing.

I rise and manage to hack off one of the scorpion's thinner back legs and it loses its balance. Jumping again to strike I see the woman's face on top of its head. She has red eyes and black lips. The skin is ghastly and paper thin. She smiles at me and screams a thousand screams threatening my ears to bleed. Her teeth are yellow and mangled. Without a second thought I put the blade in between her eyes and the creature falls over in a heap and turns into more dunes of garbage.

"Riku!" Hajime is running towards me.

"Hajime, are you alright?" I ask.

"Yes. What about you?"

"I'm fine."

I should thank him for saving me but I don't. We continue through the mounds of disposed flesh and lizards in silence.

***

There are doors leading to nowhere and doors on the ceiling. Some are locked. Others open but have no stairs or any way of safely entering. We see chimeras fighting each other to death and rooms filled with glowing red orbs and nothing else. Entering any door seems dangerous but I have to save her. We keep going. Hajime and I open one after another. I'm frustrated. I miss Aiya. She always sought me out and I abandoned her more than once. How could I think I was better than her father? I am just as bad as him. Maybe I deserve to be down here. I'm a horrible person.

"Riku?" My name being called pulls me from my thoughts.

"Yes?"

"Why didn't you come back for Aiya sooner?" he asks. I know his question is out of curiosity and not spite. It irritates me but I conceal my frustration and shame.

"I did once. But I was a coward. I was too afraid to approach her," I say.

"Why is that?" Hajime looks at me with great consideration. I wish to escape this situation.

"I thought she wouldn't love me back." He chuckles but not out of arrogance.

"How could you think that?"

"I didn't think someone so perfect could love someone like me," I say.

"Someone like you? What do you mean?" he asks.

"I've been many things. A son, a brother, a soldier, a disgraced prince. I've decimated armies. My father forced me to destroy and steal to honor our kingdom. I don't know how I am to fill the role of husband and father. My father was a warmonger. Our culture forces us to kill the alpha to ascend to the throne. My siblings tried to murder me for going against our traditions. I come from a brutal upbringing."

"That doesn't matter. Love transcends all things. Aiya loved you and she didn't even know it. It hurt me to see her wait by the treeline and sing about someone she only saw in her dreams."

"You heard her," I say. My statement is flat on my tongue.

"Yes."

"You must hate that she loves me." I scoff at myself. Hajime looks confused.

"Why would you think that?" he asks.

"Don't you? I am not a worthy man. She deserves better."

"You are worthy just the way you are, Riku. If you are worried that you are not good enough you should strive to do better. Don't ignore the challenges ahead of you but be confident in the fact that you two are meant to be. I have been able to see that for many years. I hope you see it one day as well," he says.

Hajime walks in front and I lag behind. I'm dumbfounded by his keen sense of sight. He can see what matters. I am lost in thought and not paying attention to my surroundings.

"I hate your sad puppy dog eyes! Just get away from me!"

"Aiya," I can't finish my sentence. The light of my life doesn't love me anymore. She tried to kill our baby. The bandage on her stomach is soaked in blood. Red ink drips from the bottom and stains the white sheets. A scarlet river runs between us.

"What is a nonbeliever? Just an outsider." Rena is snarling in my face.

"You live in a fantasy," I growl.

"No, little brother. You do. Having a child with that girl. I pity the gods that chose you for such a challenge." She flings the words at me with venom sticking to her lips. It's bittersweet and reminds me of a citrus kiss to an open cut.

"You broke your promise." Yahei is looking at me with a stony face.

"I tried...I'm sorry–" I hear myself apologize.

"You're always sorry." My little brother digs into my neck with his elbow. I can't take the pain. Dying would be better than being abused by him.

"A stray? A runt? A brother? Who am I to you?" I hear my words echoing in my mind.

"No one," says my older brother. Ryo is king. He hurls the sentence with individual shards of metal. The words cause the blood coursing in my veins to retreat. It is replaced by the rotten black goo seeping from the walls of The Underworld.

"Son," my father's voice bellows. It is harmonious and authoritative.

"Father, I–" my voice sounds shaky.

"You disappoint me."

"What?"

"You are incorrigible. A bad son, bad brother. You'd be the perfect soldier if your loyalty

was sincere. Your fake attempt at blending in is a joke. Everyone can see you are the outsider. You'll never belong."

His words are crisp. I feel tiny cuts all over my body. It stings like deadly hornets.

"No, please. Stop. I can't take it anymore..." I beg.

The truth of who I am is revealed. I am no one. I am a bad brother, son, and fiance. I won't be any good at being a husband or father. Aiya should have chosen someone else. Why me? Why did the gods give me something I don't deserve?

"Riku?" It's Hajime's voice. "Riku, can you hear me?"

What's happening? I can hear him. I can't see him. Where am I? Everything is covered in crimson dust. Everyone I've ever known hates me.

"No, Riku. They don't." It's his voice again.

"What?"

"You and Aiya have a lot in common. She couldn't see how loved she was either." *I gasp at the statement.*

"I think you are wrong. No one cares about me," *I shout.*

"That's not true. You know it's not true."

I think of all the generous people in the villages. How thankful they are of my help. They treat me like I am a god. I remember the kindness of every person I meet. Aiya's village has the kindest people I've ever met.

"What do you mean?"

"The only person who doesn't love you, Riku, is you." *The declaration causes me to open my eyes.*

"Hajime?"

"Riku! You're okay!"

"What happened to me?" I ask.

"I turned around and saw this thing sucking on your neck," he says.

Hajime shows me what looks like an eel. It has dark red eyes and jagged teeth, they are tiny but plentiful. The fins on it have blue spikes and the spine is lined with them as well. I feel my throat and am met with the incisions made by the creature.

"Thank you," I rasp.

"Nothing without you," he says.

"What?"

"That is your demonic canon, right? I heard you and your sister say it to each other." Hajime puts two fingers to his lips, then points at me.

"Yes," I say.

"I would do anything for Aiya, so I would do anything for you," he says.

"I'm sorry. I don't know what to say." I feel shy and tense.

"You don't have to say anything." Hajime keeps walking and I rub the numerous teeth marks on my neck.

***

The Underworld winds down and down. Deeper into the core of the earth. We are entering the place beyond. There is soot and ash everywhere. A river of fire lines both sides of the path. There is a lake of crimson liquid. I see limbs and organs float to the surface. The blood is a soup made by a demented soul. Teeth, ribs, and eyelids bubble in the scarlet water. It foams over the rocks.

"Hey." Kaji manifests from the steam. He sits on the ledge above us with Aiya's Wraith in his lap. She's straddling him and he has his hands all over her.

"You bastard," I growl. Hajime grabs my arm and shakes his head at me.

"I think she likes me," he says and sticks his tongue in her mouth. I see it moving in her throat. The sight chills my spine and turns it into glass. I want to take the shards and slit my wrists.

"Don't fall for it, Riku." Hajime furrows his brow.

"The wolf prince who fell in love with a young girl! Such a charming story. Too bad it won't have a happy ending," he taunts. Kaji laughs and the flames rise. The crackling noise is his voice echoing in the coals.

"I'll never let you have her," I say as I narrow my eyes at the man who holds the ghost of my beloved's soul.

"I'm not so sure about that," says Kaji, winking at me.

He picks up Aiya's Wraith and caresses her thigh while staring at me. He walks off into the nothing, his boots thud with each step, and ignite small fires. My breaths weigh heavy with sticky tar. I want to punch something. Hajime holds the collar of my bodysuit to make sure I don't run off.

"Thanks," I mumble.

There is a groaning coming from the red waves. Shadow men rise and make their way towards us. Hajime is skilled with a sword and cuts them down with prowess. The only problem is there are too many. Countless shadowy beings emerge and head in our direction. We slice through them and they turn to black mist. They scream as they evaporate. A terrible acrid scent coats the inside of my bloody nose causing it to twitch. I push down the panic. There is no time for such a luxury. I have to keep him safe.

"Hajime!" I call his name and he comes to my side. We stand back to back.

"Riku, do you trust me?" he asks. I don't know if I do.

"Yes," I say.

The words leave my lips and Hajime pushes me back. He swings the sword in a wide motion. It glows bright pink and white. The blade strikes the dead shadow puppets with pink lightning. It tears through their bodies and the mist is a dark cloud around us. He turns around and strikes the ground, more pink lightning ripping the black souls into bits.

The lightning ricochets off the walls and slices through the shadow men. More of them rise from the river of lava but he is able to cut them down without my help. They come at us in hordes but he only has to strike a few times to decimate the army of dark souls.

"Hajime, how did you do that?" I ask in disbelief. He was able to defeat the army of shadow men on his own.

"I do not fight with my bodily strength," he says as he touches his chest. "I use my heart. I aim with someone I love in mind," he says. Hajime looks at me with a grave expression.

"We should continue. I hope we're getting close."

We walk without words for quite some time. The rodents of The Underworld sneak glances at us from their hiding places in the moist walls. It sweats down here. Everything is wet and the air is humid. I see Hajime pick up his bangs and spy the salt of his sweat on his brow and hairline.

There are platforms moving with no determinable pattern and staircases floating up and down. I strategize the safest route for us to go. Hajime stays by my side. I pretend to be fearless but I'm clueless. Thinking about Aiya and the way she looked when I proposed to her comforts me. The memory is perfect. Aiya, with flowers in her hair, happy. Wanting to marry me. It's subtle but I see what looks like a gold thread move past me and towards a red brick platform. I follow it and the thread leads us to an iron staircase going down towards the lake of crimson soup filled with body parts.

"Riku?"

"Just trust me," I say.

The staircase drops us off on another platform that floats, suspended in air. The gold thread rolls towards a ledge with three doors. One is red with a gold door knob. The second one is black and blue with a silver door knob. The last one is ruby and red with a messy insignia scribbled on it. It isn't ink, it's the toxic blood. This is where the gold thread stops.

I open the red door with a black symbol on it. There is no light but I have a feeling this is where we are supposed to go. Our feet wade through warm liquid we can't see. I hear a caw and then a hiss. Our steps echo in the dank atmosphere. The dim light gives everything a bloody hue. Reaching out I feel for Hajime and make sure he is right next to me. We take a turn and I almost fall to my knees. It's Aiya's Wraith.

She's in a wall glowing bright red. Her creamy skin stands out against the midnight tones of The Underworld. Rosy lips pout. Her butterfly eyelashes don't flutter. It looks like swirling scarlet water envelops her. The Wraith resides within a horrible crimson womb. Hajime and I approach. Aiya floats out of reach, her hair wrapping around her. How I long to take the inky locks and fold it around my wrist. I reach for her but the wall rejects me. The pain is abrupt and sharp. I try again but it won't let me anywhere near her. Hajime attempts to touch her as well and it stops him from getting near. I collapse and fall into myself.

"Aiya," I whisper. Hajime kneels down next to me. I can't meet his gaze.

"Riku, do you have her ring?" he asks.

"Yes," I say. My voice is raspy. I pull her ring from my pocket. The tremor in my hand is back. Hajime covers the ring in my hand with his.

"Pray with me," he orders.

"What should I pray for?" I ask.

"Pray for Aiya. Pray for your baby."

With that he closes his eyes. There are creases in his forehead. I can tell he is concentrating. I haven't prayed since I left home. I don't recite the first part but I say the last part over and over.

* * *

Nothing without you.
Nothing without you.
I
Am
Nothing
Without
You

I open my eyes to the brilliant light building between our palms. Hajime keeps his eyes closed and focused. I continue to pray but I stare at the scene unfolding before me. Aiya's Wraith wakes up. Her eyes glow bright white this time. Hajime takes the ring from my palm and stands up. He is able to cross the barrier. The darkness recoils at his presence. Reaching for her she floats down. He pulls Aiya's Wraith out of The Underworld's tomb. Around him is an ethereal glow. I would say he looks like a god.

The walls of The Underworld begin to crumble. The ceiling drips and red rain falls down. It soaks our hair and our clothes but we keep running. The blood is heavy on my eyelashes. Hot scarlet slime flows down my face and drips down my collar. There are shadow men in our way but I think of Aiya's voice saying she loves me and I am able to emit the powerful lightning, annihilating an army in one hit.

We dash past the blinking eyes crusted with disease. The cawing of crows hammers against my temples but I ignore it. The breaths I take are short and unsatisfying but the hope of feeling Aiya's arms around me encourages me to push past every uncomfortable feeling. It frustrates me that Hajime is the one carrying her but I accept. I can accept anything if I can be with her again.

Once there are no demons closing in on us I untie my sister's hair from my wrist. I wrap my arms around Hajime and Aiya's Wraith. Then I whisper into the silky white *bring me to life* and close my eyes. First nothing happens. The boulders around us fall into the hot lava below. It destroys everything it splashes. Bloody rain coats our faces. I look down to see Hajime with his eyes closed. I try to have faith as I close mine. Right when I think we are stuck down here I feel Yama's cool hand on mine.

CHAPTER TEN

The Wolf was Once Lonely

"Is everyone alright?" Yama is motherly and concerned.

"Yes." My voice is breathless. Hajime and I heave and pant. I'm sure we are quite a sight because our faces are covered in blood. Our clothes are drenched in the red liquid.

"Come with me." My sister ushers us to the hot spring where she froze Aiya.

She removes the love of my life with great care and hands her to me. The three of us communicate with our eyes and we run towards the village. Once we are at Aiya's house my sister fetches the monk and the priestess.

"Hajime, put the Wraith over Aiya," instructs the monk. He does as he is told. The Wraith floats for a moment but sinks into Aiya's body. She gasps and spits up water. I turn her to her side. Her body is plagued by violent shivers. I rip off her wet clothes and wrap her in the blanket on her bed. Lady Kiyori hands me a towel to dry her hair. She is still shaking but not as bad. Everyone looks at me with anxious eyes.

I place my palm on the stars below her navel. There is nothing. I wait for a moment. This can't be. No heartbeat, no pulse. I wait. I keep waiting until I can't. My heart breaks and even though I'm overjoyed Aiya is alive I am sad my baby is not. I watch as the faces of my sister, Hajime, the monk, and the priestess all change when the tears fall from my face and land on the bridge of Aiya's nose.

Unable to contain myself I begin to sob. I pull her close to my chest and keep my hand on her flat stomach. We were supposed to be a family. I'm sure she won't love me anymore after this. Sympathetic stares surround me as I scan the room. I hang my head and close my eyes. Then there is a cool smooth hand over mine. It's Yama. She gives me a pious look and begins to pray. The monk takes off his necklace and puts it around his wrist. He rests his palm over Yama's. The priestess joins as she places a reassuring hand on my elbow.

Hajime is the alpha, the true hero, a god. He puts his hand on top. I feel Aiya blow hot air into my neck. She is my everything. I am nothing without her. This baby would have been our everything. I keep touching her starry skin. I can't let go.

I bury my face in her hair. Everyone's hands weigh heavy on my palm and I open my eyes to see a peachy glow around Aiya's navel. I watch in amazement at the spiritual power they have as a collective. Their expressions are tranquil. A miracle happens. It isn't very strong but I feel it. A pulse below the surface of the stars. I choke on my joy and cough. Everyone looks at my face and smiles one by one.

"How did you do that?" I ask in awe.

"The gods wanted them to live," says Yama. Everyone nods in agreement.

"You two need rest. I will bring you food in a little bit," says the priestess. She gets up and so do the others.

"Hajime, wait," I say. He stops in the doorway and turns around.

"Yes?"

"How did you pull Aiya's Wraith out of The Underworld?"

"We prayed for her."

"But what were you saying in your prayer?" My question causes him to smile that thoughtful grin.

"I prayed for her to remember your name," he says.

With that he hands me her ring. He exits Aiya's house and we are alone. I look down at her and admire the freckles on her face. They are visible again. I uncover her navel and notice there are more stars on her stomach. The gash is gone and there is a new constellation. I lean down and kiss it.

I get into bed with Aiya and press my ear to her heart. The sound brings on a wave of joy and I find myself smiling with my teeth. It vanishes as soon as I think about my behavior. How I made her feel about the baby. The way I would disappear on her. I am protective and curl around her. It's not necessary but it makes me feel better.

"Aiya...I'm so sorry. I will never leave you. Not a day will go by where I am not by your side. I will stay right here until you tell me to go. There will never be a time where I hide from you again. If you call my name I will come running. I love you more than anything. Please, forgive me." I scoot down and fall asleep to the sound of Aiya's heart communicating with our baby's.

***

The wolf was once lonely
But never again
He is my one
He is my only
We were once two
Now we're a family

It seems too good to be true. It must be a dream. I wake up to Aiya singing about me in her beautiful voice.

"Aiya." I look up to see her smiling at me.

"Hi," she whispers. I kiss her and she puts her arms around me.

"I thought I lost you," I say as I take a handful of black ink into my palm.

She touches my face and rubs her nose with mine even though I am covered in blood. Her face changes and I feel the air turn chilly in my lungs.

"Riku, I did such an ugly thing. I am so sorry. Can you ever forgive me?" she asks. Aiya covers her face and sobs. I hold her and run my hand along her spine to soothe her.

"Don't say sorry. I know your heart. That wasn't you," I say.

"I love our baby. You have to know how much I want them."

Her body trembles from violent sobs. I pull away and kiss her face a hundred times.

"I know you do. You loved them first."

I put my palm back over her starry stomach. The pulse is a little stronger. She smiles even though it looks like it pains her to do so. She wraps herself around me and we lay like that until Lady Kiyori knocks at the door.

"Come in," says Aiya. The priestess brings us clear soup with vegetables and rice.

"Thank you," I say.

"You're welcome. How are you feeling, Aiya?" asks Lady Kiyori.

"Kind of dizzy." Her voice is weak but it's still beautiful.

"You'll feel better after you eat. What about you, Riku?" The priestess looks at me with curiosity.

"I'm good. I'm happy to have my family back," I say. My answer causes both Aiya and the priestess to give each other a sly grin.

"Good. I'm glad. Oh, I forgot to give you this," she says. The priestess hands me Aiya's yellow and spider lily kimono. There are no blood stains. It looks new.

"I thought this was ruined. Thank you," I say.

"I have a little magic of my own," says Lady Kiyori.

She winks at me and this makes me feel like we are sharing a secret. Aiya giggles and kisses my neck. "You two probably want to be alone. I'll check on you tomorrow."

The priestess glides out the door, the paper ribbon shaking in her hair. Aiya presses against me. She is listening to my heart, my chin rests on top of her head, my palm is on the stars of her navel.

"Riku, do you want to know what our baby looks like?" asks Aiya. She sits up and touches my hand that is over her stomach. I think about it for a moment. I want them to look just like her.

"No. I want it to be a surprise."

This pleases Aiya and she lays back down with me.

"I love you," she says.

"I love you, too."

"Riku?"

"Yes?"

"It was Hanako who told me your name. That's how I knew it."

"I am forever indebted to Hanako," I sigh.

"I can't wait to tell her that I'm pregnant." Aiya's eyes are closed. Her face is serene.

"She's going to be really happy."

"We're all going to be really happy," she says.

***

I step outside and enjoy the fragrance of fresh snow. Aiya is sleeping but I want to watch snowflakes fall from the heavens for a moment. I feel different. Every worry I had has been erased. Nothing will be easy but I'm confident I am up to the challenge. Aiya singing to me this morning makes me smile to myself. I am content letting the snow collect in my hair.

"Riku?" says Haru. I look over to see Yuta's wife staring up at me.

"Haru, what are you doing here?"

"I wanted to come say hi."

She smiles and it brings out her dimple. I turn my gaze away but catch glimpses of the magic copper laced bark and sunshine.

"Hi," I whisper. The young girl makes me skittish. I'm not sure why. The sky is gray but there is a cheerful atmosphere in the village today. Perhaps it is just me.

"Can I ask you something?"

"Sure," I say.

"I know I already asked but can I touch your hair again? Please?" she asks. Haru is petite. Shorter than Aiya who barely comes to my chest. I would look to Aiya for permission but I want Haru to be my friend so I kneel down. I'm sure Aiya won't mind.

"Okay." My voice is softer than usual. Yuta's wife uses her tiny hand to brush the bangs from my face. She is closer than I anticipated, analyzing me with chestnut eyes. Her top lip pouts but I can tell she is a happy girl. She catches me off guard by placing her other hand on my cheek.

"Wow," she gasps.

"What?" I ask.

"You are very beautiful but don't know it. I think that makes you more beautiful."

The young girl's statement causes me to flinch. She pulls her hands back and giggles. I wish to say something but I can't. Running off back towards her house she looks over her shoulder to wave and smile at me. I realize why Haru makes me nervous. She reminds me of

Aiya the day I heard her sing about me.

***

Aiya is my air, my everything. She melted the ice in my heart. I am the rain but she is the storm. There nights I look to the moon and want to howl. I wish for the wolf god to answer me. *Why am I the one?* I am grateful. No one will ever love her the way I love her. Aiya looks good in every color but she is my summer in yellow. The days where she wears blue she is my dream, my storm, the ocean I drown in. Aiya's heart is my heart and she is the embers in red. I fall asleep listening to two hearts beat in one. They communicate in a language I don't understand but it is music to my ears.

We walk hand in hand and sleep in each other's arms. This time I allow her to love me. To really love me. Sitting next to her I could disappear and be in one hundred places at once. I don't anymore. There is no moment with her that isn't important. I want to know everything about her. Her favorite color is red. She loves spider lilies. Aiya drinks jasmine green tea and prefers sunrises over sunsets. The birds wait for her to sing to them as do I. The spirits of the forest can't look away from her as she dances with flowers in her hair. The breeze picks up her long black tresses as she stares up at the sky.

"What are you thinking about?" I ask.

"How my life has changed. I thought I had no family but my family keeps growing. I'm lucky," she whispers.

"We both are."

PART TWO

Remember You

CHAPTER ELEVEN

Disappearing Ink

Hanako and I race through the forest faster than lightning. We are able to run past wild horses and beat the deer to the treeline. Her delicate nose twitches as she laughs. I smile all the time now. Riku is chasing us. He doesn't like this game.

The summer heat scorches the ground. It's lava on my feet but I feel no pain. The fox princess and I are kindred spirits, two sisters, one soul. I am in love with the wolf and he is my everything. After my father died, I stopped living. I didn't know what I was waiting for at the time but I realized it's been him all along. I am resurrected.

"Aiya! Wait!" Riku calls for me but Hanako and I fling off our bright colored kimonos and jump.

The cliff leads to still dark water. It reminds me of Chiyo's eyes. I break the surface, sinking into the depths where it is more black than blue. Opening my eyes I can see the silver bodies in the darkness. Purple and indigo shapes move through the water. It's almost like they're dancing. I feel arms around me and let out bubbles giggling to the surface.

"Aiya! What are you doing?" The wolf prince looks at me bewildered as I laugh up the liquid in my lungs.

I cover my mouth with one hand and have the other on his shoulder. Riku stares at me for a moment but he laughs when I laugh. It's a wonderful sound.

"Having fun," I say and kiss him. He guides me out of the blue green and hands me his cloak without looking at me.

"Here, you can dry yourself with this."

"I don't mind if you look at me." I take the cloak but he remains turned away.

"I mind." He's walking off without me. Not wanting to offend him I cover myself up and follow.

"Riku! Aiya! That was amazing," exclaims Hanako. She is shaking the water off her adorable red and black ears. Riku seems embarrassed and hands us our kimonos without a glance. "Thank you," she says.

Her pretty hands wipe the water from her cheeks. The canines in her mouth are sharp but her smile is inviting. It's light pink, the color of magnolias. She is never embarrassed.

"You're welcome," he mumbles.

Hanako and I try not to giggle but we exchange a look and grin. I don't think Riku has ever had a friend. He is baffled by our kindness towards him. We get him to play games with us though. There are times he doesn't want to smile but we find ways to get him to grin. The wolf doesn't know what to say but I talk enough for both of us.

"I'm having so much fun with you. Are you having fun with me?" I ask as I pick a lily for Riku. He stops in his tracks.

"Yes, of course," he says. I take his hand and we make our way through the endless cedars and oak trees. Hanako picks up acorns littering the mossy ground.

"What are you doing?" I ask her.

"Watch," she says. Hanako takes the handful of acorns and whispers into them with her magnolia mouth. She sets them down and they become tiny horses. They rear up and run across the dirt. I get on my knees to see them better. They make the slight "nay" sound and run in a pack.

"Wow," I say. My voice is breathless.

I'm learning more everyday. There is a lot to remember. I want to know everything about Riku. It comforts me to know we will have forever. Riku kneels down to put his arm around me. I touch his handsome face. His eyes are honey amber, light gold. They are stunning but sad. The wolf has puppy dog eyes despite being a soldier and a hero. I would never say so out loud and tuck it away into the quiet of my thoughts.

"This is beautiful, Hanako," he says.

Anytime Riku speaks, Hanako and I turn to him in wonder. He doesn't say a lot but he is meaningful when he does. The demon fox princess and the wolf prince from the north seem to have an unspoken bond.

"Thank you, Riku. I like making people happy with magic," she beams.

After a few moments the horses return to acorns. He helps me to my feet and we continue through the green abyss. This is where I live now. I love it here. I love being with him.

There are chubby robins. Orange and black feathers announce their presence on a low hanging branch. They are watching us. I stop and tilt my head back. From my lips rings the song of the birds. Riku watches me with intensity. I think this interests him because he doesn't look away.

The robins watch me with shiny eyes. In a long and haunting tone they answer. They sing to me as I sing to them. This pleases Hanako and she jumps with delight. Once more I call out to them and they call back.

"How did you do that?" asks Riku. He takes my hands in his and looks at me.

"What was her name?" He hasn't asked many questions.

"Hatsumomo." Saying my mother's name I exhale pink air. I miss her.

"Was she beautiful like you?"

Riku and I keep walking. Hanako never goes too far but I see her chasing a squirrel. It makes chirping noises as it evades her.

"More beautiful. Men fell to their knees for her. My father proposed to her on her seventeenth birthday. She had received six other marriage proposals but she was waiting for him," I say. As the story leaves my lips I feel Riku grab me and pull me close.

"What about your mother, Riku?"

"She was cold and distant. Yuna was pretty to look at but poisonous." I wish to ask more questions but I don't want to upset him.

"My mother was wonderful. She sang to the birds everyday.

After a while they refused to sing until she joined them. I saw her pet a red deer once. It was bounding through the field but it stopped to let her touch him. My father would come home and every night she would say, 'There you are. I've been waiting for you.' It's my favorite memory of them."

I sense I am making Riku uncomfortable talking about my family. His arms go slack and I take his hand again.

"Are you happy with me?" he asks. His question is a clawed hand around my heart. I stop in my tracks.

"Of course. I love being with you." I kiss him and he turns up the corners of his mouth but doesn't give me a true smile.

"Really?" he asks. The wolf demon wears heavy armor and has fought in many wars but is most shy around me.

"Yes, really."

"You can tell me if you aren't."

"I love you," I say. This seems to make him feel better. I pull back his bangs so I can really look at him. The sad puppy dog eyes get me every time and I kiss him until Hanako comes back.

***

It's the middle of the night but I have crystal clear vision. Hanako and I are playing hide and seek. Riku doesn't like this game either but he plays anyway. I am hiding up high in a cedar. Hanako is shielding herself with fern leaves and using her magic to blend in. I watch as Riku searches for us and cover my mouth to keep my giggle from escaping.

He is tall and handsome. I have almond shaped eyes, his are a wider set, resembling the sad eyes of a canine. There is something sweet about his face. People are intimidated by him but not me. I see the kindness no one bothers to look for. Riku doesn't find us. I can't take it anymore so I slide down the tree and sneak up behind him.

"Gotcha!" I surprise him with a kiss.

"I'm right here," says Hanako as she pops out from a fern to his left. Riku appears startled and I feel bad.

I don't think he is used to constant company or playing games. I take his hand so we can walk together. The stars are bright in the sky.

They remind me of Hanako's hair.

The three of us exit the treeline and come upon a grassy knoll of wildflowers. The moon is full and there's a summer breeze filled with the floral scent of the hillside. Hanako begins picking the long stems and wandering further down. Riku stands still and admires the sky.

"What are you thinking about?" I ask.

"I was looking at the moon and wondering about the wolf god," he says. The shadows of his face contour the well sculpted cheekbones and jawline. I lay in the grass and pull Riku down with me. Staring up at the sky I wonder who it is watching over me. I could have died in the village but I didn't. Who was it who chose Riku? Why did they want me to live?

We watch the same sky but we are not in the same place. Riku is somehow next to me but in one hundred different places at once. I often feel like I am waiting for him to come back to me even though he already has. The wind shakes the flowers and it rains pink and white. I pick a white flower, the biggest one, and hand it to Riku.

"Do you like flowers?" I ask. He takes the flower with care and stares at it, analyzing it like it has a secret.

"Do you like flowers?" he asks. I reach for a pink one and place it behind my ear.

"I love flowers."

"Then I like flowers," he says. Riku's answer is sincere but it makes me sad he won't tell me how he feels. Hanako returns with an armful of the orange, pink, and white blossoms. Dark green stems with oval leaves stick out from her wrists.

"Look how many I got!" Hanako gives us a wide grin.

The moonlight shines in her hair and it shimmers. She sits next to us and begins weaving the flowers together into floral crowns. Placing the first one on me with a sweet face I can't help but laugh with joy. I feel even happier watching Hanako place one on Riku. He doesn't reject it. In fact I think the wolf demon is blushing.

"Thanks Hanako," he says in his quiet but gruff voice.

"Do you like it?" she asks.

"Yes." His answer makes Hanako happy and she hugs him.

"Aiya, how do you like living out here with us?" she asks.

"I love it!" I say, twirling another pink flower in my hand.

Petals fly off and drift down into my lap.

"Do you want to go back home?" she asks. Hanako is always checking on me.

"No, not yet. I am having too much fun."

I look over to see Riku watching me. He looks down when we make eye contact. Hanako moves closer to me and starts braiding my hair. It's grown past my waist. She adorns the thick black ink with tiny orange and white blossoms. Touching my face she sighs.

"You're so beautiful." Her voice is waves breaking against the sand.

"Thank you," I whisper. She gets up to dance around the field in her unique and lively way. I scoot closer to Riku and brush his hair back.

"Hi," he says. For some reason this stokes the embers of my heart and I find myself never wanting to stop looking at him.

"Hi," I giggle and kiss his cheek. The wolf demon puts his arms around me. I feel him play with my hair and wrap it around his wrist. The moon is full above us and I peek at it wondering if the wolf god is watching me, too.

Riku and I admire the night sky together. I steal glances of him looking up at the moon. We are finally together. The remedy I needed but didn't know existed. Where does he go as we sit in silence? Do we pray for the same things? What did I do to deserve someone that resembles a god?

"I love you," he says. Riku always says it back but rarely says it first.

"I love you. I've loved you for a long time," I say. I was hoping my answer would make him happy but he seems hurt. I wonder what I said?

"How long?"

"I didn't know why I felt empty. I assumed it was because of what happened to me and my family. After I started my search for you something became apparent."

"What's that?" he asks.

"That I had been looking for you since I was sixteen."

I give him a kiss to make him feel better but he is stiff. My lips have no effect on him. I retreat into myself and turn my gaze to the tall grass blowing in the wind. We don't speak for what feels like a hundred years. I wish I didn't say anything.

"I'm sorry," he says. I'm confused and it must be written on my face.

"For what?" I ask.

"I should have come back for you sooner. I'm sorry."

"Don't be sorry. I'm not mad."

I offer him a warm look but he vanishes, disappearing ink I can never read in time.

***

The sun rises. The yellow orb reveals itself after the moon and the wolf god return to their spectral plain. Hanako is sleeping behind me. I look over my shoulder to see her ears twitching as she dreams. Her green and pink kimono is bright and cheery. It suits her. Riku and I sleep tangled up in each other.

The sleeves of my kimono bunch up at my elbows. My freckled skin is fair but not as fair as Riku's. He is a beautiful ghost. There are times I worry I'll wake up and he won't be here. His expression is relaxed as he sleeps. No longer tense from his thoughts he dreams in peace while I run my fingers through his snowy hair. I've never seen anything like it. He is pine needles and ice. I would freeze in the harshest winter if it was the only way to be with him.

"Aiya," he whispers my name in his sleepy voice and my heart flutters. He kisses me and I close my eyes. Not feeling close enough I press against him.

"Good morning," I yawn.

"Good morning." Riku traces my spine with his hand.

"Did you sleep well?" I ask.

"Yes. Did you?" I know he is wondering about my nightmares.

"Yes. I don't have bad dreams anymore," I say.

We go back to sleep in each other's web. We must have slept for a long time because Hanako is shaking us awake.

"C'mon guys! You've been sleeping half the day. Let's go," she exclaims.

Riku and I get up and follow the fox princess. She guides us to a blue green lake surrounded by hydrangeas and daisies. Hanako and I rip off our kimonos without a care. As we enter the water I smell the freshness of the flowers mixed with the clear aquatic notes. Riku stands at the edge and watches over us.

"Are you going to join me?" I ask.

"I'm okay," he says. I want him to swim with me but I don't want to pester him. I nod to show I accept his answer but my heart is frayed. My sad feeling is diminished as Hanako comes up from the bottom and squirts water at me.

"Hey!" I put my arms up and laugh.

My collar bone is exposed and I catch Riku looking at it. He isn't innocent but he is chivalrous. Since my transformation I have been uninhibited. In my old life I would have never thrown off my kimono and jumped into the blue green. Now I do what makes me feel alive. I am free.

"What are you going to do about it?" teases Hanako.

"I'm going to get you!"

I chase her across the lake. We splash and play in the blue green reminding me of the obi Riku wears. Hanako dives underneath where I can't see her. I take a deep breath and explore the lake myself. There are magnificent koi. They are cute and chubby. Marbled bodies are shades of red, orange, and white. I reach out and they let me pet their unearthly bodies. A baby koi the size of my palm swims against my flat stomach. The fins tickle below my navel where I have a splash of freckles.

The koi are playing in my hair. It is a curtain of black ink and they weave through the tresses. I reach into the long dark locks and they tickle my wrists. My arms have freckles at the elbows. I am a starry night in the depths below.

A giant koi, bigger than the others, swims in front of me. It looks at me and I notice it has a horn on its head. I am new to this world but I think this is the king koi. He has black and gold spots mixing with the crimson sunset. There are arms around me pulling me away from the amazing sight.

"Aiya!" Riku is shaking me.

"What?" I ask.

"You scared me! What are you doing?" he shouts. I know he

worries. He worries too much and I don't know how to make him feel better.

"I'm sorry. I was admiring the koi."

I feel myself shrinking in Riku's presence. Unsure of what to do I kiss him. This seems to confuse him but he lets me go.

"It's okay," he mumbles and exits the lake.

His cloak is soaking wet and drips from the hem. The armor he wears is incredible but heavy. He must be so strong to be able to swim with it on. Hanako glides through the water next to me. Her face says she saw the whole thing. We wait for Riku to disappear into the treeline.

"Don't be mad at Riku. This is new for him. He loves you very much." Her cheery face is serious but kind.

"I'm not mad. I'm a little sad, though. I just want him to be happy. I thought he would be..." I trail off.

"He is. But this is special. So special. He knows that and I think that's why is scared," says Hanako.

"Why would he be scared?"

"Riku wandered the forest alone for over a decade, Aiya. Love may be difficult for him. I know he loves you with all his heart," she says while looking at the passing clouds with a dreamy expression.

"How do you know?" I ask. I am certain he loves me but I am curious what Hanako sees that I do not.

"The night before we reached your village I saw him cry. He was really happy to see you again but couldn't tell you." My friend's admission makes my heart ache and sink to the bottom of the lake.

"After I fell off the cliff and saw his face I knew what I had been searching for. All the times I tried to fill the gnawing emptiness inside but couldn't find the cure. I needed to see his gold eyes," I say.

"I'm happy you two are together."

"Me too."

CHAPTER TWELVE

The Games We Play for Keeps

Autumn is here and she brings with her red, orange, and yellow paint. She changes the leaves and they fall. I reach for Riku but feel nothing but the crunch of a maple leaf. Opening my eyes I see he is gone. Hanako is sleeping. It looks like she is chasing something in her dream.

I get up in search of him. He does this to me on occasion. Worried I may never see him again, I race through the forest. I can't find him or smell the familiar scent of pine needles and ice. Where did he go? The sun is rising in the east and the shadows begin to disappear.

My heart beats slower with sadness. Feeling defeated I find a patch of sun to sit in. I pull my kimono up to my thigh and tie the hem. Riku hates how I do this but I want to be able to run faster.

"Hey," a gravelly voice speaks to me from up in the tree.

I crane my head to see a man with short wavy black hair. He appears human but has shiny black and brown ears on top of his head. A jaguar demon. His chest is broad and covered in dark hair. It's around his navel, too. Black spots mark his pecs and shoulders. He wears no shoes or shirt, only black trousers covering his muscular body.

"Hi." I don't feel like talking to this man.

"What's a pretty girl like you doing all by yourself?" he purrs.

"Looking for my lover," I say. I'm hoping bringing up that I'm with someone will deter the cat. It doesn't.

"Why is he avoiding you? I would be by your side every minute, of every day if I were him," he purrs. The jaguar smiles and his feline fangs sparkle like ivory.

"He's not avoiding me."

"Looks like he is to me."

The jaguar demon is getting on my nerves. I gaze into his emerald eyes and see them roaming up and down my body. I don't say anything. "What? Cat got your tongue?" he roars with laughter.

"Just go away," I hiss.

"I can tell by the look in your eyes that you want to be mine. Lover boy keeps you waiting, doesn't he?" The cat winks at me. Are all feline demons this salacious?

"No," I say in a cold voice.

"Come here," he growls.

The jaguar drops from the tree and makes his way towards me, "I see it in your burning red eyes. A desire deep inside. You want me. C'mon, be mine." The energy shifts and I feel someone behind me.

"She's mine," Riku barks and draws his sword. I look up to see his serious but handsome face. He's baring his canines at the jaguar demon.

"Hey there, lover boy. You got here just in time. She was about to give into me," taunts the jaguar.

Riku charges at him but he jumps into the tree and vanishes without a sound. He's panting and seems really upset.

"I'm sorry," my voice is small as he helps me to my feet.

"Don't say you're sorry."

Riku and I walk back to where Hanako is sleeping. He hasn't said a word to me. I worry I did something wrong. Riku eyes my short kimono and I contemplate untying it but don't. There is the crunching of leaves as we lay down and we enjoy the last of the sunrise together. The yellow orb glows white in his gold eyes.

"Where do you go?" I ask.

"To be by myself," he says.

"Do you not like being with me?" He seems hurt by my question.

"I love you. I love being with you. It's an old habit. I'm sorry," he kisses me. I feel like he is going to leave again so I cling to him.

"I love you." I'm pulling at the collar of his shirt. I should let go but I can't.

"What's wrong?" He holds me in his strong arms but I feel alone.

"I get scared you're not going to come back," I say.

"I would never leave you. Never."

"You promise?"

"I promise," he says.

I kiss his neck and wait for him to fall asleep so I can relax. It's the only time I feel like he is really with me.

***

The waning crescent moon is so close I think I can touch it. The night flowers are blooming. They smell like dew and honey. The breeze is cool but it's refreshing. I'm burning up but I'm not ill. In the shadows of a camphor tree I look down the grassy hill to see Hanako sitting next to Riku.

I don't think he's ever had a friend. I am glad he has Hanako. She is a kindhearted and pure person. There is an orange flower to her left. She picks only the head, leaving the stem. Closing the delicate blossom between her pretty hands she whispers to it. Something sweet happens. She opens her palm to reveal a butterfly.

Riku looks at it with curiosity. It flies from her hand landing on his nose. This makes him flinch but the magic butterfly remains. Hanako claps and giggles. Riku stares at the magnificent creature and smiles. My heart bursts and I feel as though I won't be able to contain the love spilling out behind my sternum. Placing my palm over my chest I try my best to keep it inside. The pressure is enormous but it isn't painful. Hanako reaches for the butterfly and it turns back into a flower. She places it in his hand and skips off. Riku stares at the blossom then turns his gaze to the stars.

"Hi." I put my arms around his neck.

"Hi," he says.

Riku is still looking at the stars. I study him staring up at the night sky and try to piece together what he is thinking about.

"Riku, do you like stars?" I ask.

He is quiet for an eternity but he answers. The wolf prince is touching my cheeks, the bridge of my nose, and the corner of my lip.

"I love stars. They remind me of your freckles," he says. His words steal my breath. I can't talk so I smile and kiss his face a hundred times. Riku is difficult to read but I think he's happy.

"No one else in my family had freckles," I say, not expecting a reply.

"You are the girl with stars on her face. The gods made you special," he says.

Riku is over a century old. I know he communicates with the spirits of the forest and understands the intricacies of demons. Who am I to the wolf god? How does one receive a message from the heavens? I wonder if he's right.

"You think so?" I ask.

"I know so."

***

"Hanako, can I ask you a question?"

"Of course. What is it, Aiya?"

The fox princess and I are bathing in a hot spring. There are boulders and saplings surrounding us. Stray camellias bloom pink and red, contrasting against the brown and yellow hues. Riku didn't want to join us and has gone off on his own.

"What do you know about wolf demons?" I look into the clear water and feel the steam swirl around my face.

"Not too much. I know their culture is brutal, very strict. It's unusual for them to leave the pack. They are known to be fiercely loyal. Protective," she says. Hanako washes her furry ears and wrings water from her sparkly hair.

"What do you mean by loyal?" I stand up to pick a flower from between the rocks and pluck at the petals, littering red ovals into the hot spring.

"Wolves have little for themselves. Everything they do is for the pack."

"Oh," I trail off not knowing what to say.

"You are Riku's pack now. He will never leave you," she says. Her declaration cheers me up but I'm still unsure.

"He left his family, his home, his whole life. Who is to say one day he won't wake up and leave me, too?" I haven't said it outloud and hearing the horrible words makes me cringe. Hanako's ears turn downwards and her bright expression fades.

"You can't believe that, Aiya. Riku would never do that to you."

"How do you know?" I am getting irritated but don't want to be mean to my friend.

"I just know. I saw him wandering alone a couple of times. His face was so sorrowful. I thought he was beautiful but it made me sad to see the hurt in his eyes. Now that you are in his life he smiles. Maybe not all the time but he does at least once a day. His face lights up when he sees you. I never saw him look at anything or anyone the way he looks at you," Hanako's magnolia mouth utters such wonderful things.

My insecurity threatens to consume me. I try to push it out of my mind and believe the fox princess.

"Hanako, have you ever been in love?" I ask. She smiles but it has a hint of grief.

"Yes. I've been in love numerous times but my biggest love was a human boy named Hinote. He was my first love."

"You fell in love with a human?" I stop torturing the flowers to look at her.

"I did. His mother hated me. She despised the idea of a union between a human and demon. We were both young. I understand better now but at the time I was distraught."

"What do you understand now?" I wonder if Riku and I would be in love if I were still human.

"Why she hated me. She thought I was a bad demon. Hinote's parents called us filthy dogs. It was a cruel thing to say. She was right about one thing, though."

"What's that?" I wring the water from my hair and listen intently to her tell me the story of her first love.

"That it would have been unfair," she says.

"How so?" I ask.

"Because he would have loved me all his life but I would have many loves after his life ended." I'm amazed by Hanako's deep insight.

"I never thought about it like that," I admit, feeling strange about my own heart.

"I didn't either until I got older. Now I'm happy we didn't stay together." Hanako stretches and her slender arms are milky white against the autumn tones.

"You are?"

"Yes. He got married to a human woman and had three children. If we had a family they would be a hundred years old and he would have been gone long ago."

"I understand," I whisper.

Riku, would you have been happier if I married Hajime instead?

***

Riku is sitting by himself admiring the cedars and the oak trees. The valley is beautiful this time of year. Red is my favorite color even though it reminds me of Kasai. I still love it. The maple leaves combined with the changing orange and yellow hues has me pause an extra moment. I sneak up behind him and cover his eyes with my hands.

"Guess who," I whisper. He holds my wrists but not tight.

"I don't think I understand this game." His voice isn't very loud but it's rough. I uncover his eyes and kiss him.

"Games are just for fun. You don't have to understand them." I give him a reassuring smile.

"You really like to play games," he says.

"Yeah, I guess I do. I didn't used to."

"Really?" Riku doesn't ask me many questions and I am flattered when he does.

"I spent most of my time alone," I admit.

"Why?" I feel my ears turn pink at his question. This must be awful for him to hear.

"I didn't think anyone cared about me," I say. Riku wants to say more but he doesn't. We sit with the sound of the autumn breeze shaking the leaves out of the trees.

"I don't know how you could think that," he mumbles.

"What?" I know what he said but I want him to speak up.

"I don't know how you could think that," he repeats. I shrug. It's hard to explain, even to myself.

"It doesn't matter now." Riku nods and surprises me by laying in my lap. I run my hands through his hair, silk and snowflakes.

"Will you sing to me?" he asks. I feel my face flush but it makes me happy.

> *The wolf was once lonely*
> *But never again*
> *He is my one*
> *He is my only*

Riku perks up at this and kisses me hard, much harder than usual. It makes my heart race and steals my breath.

"Did you like my song for you?"

I am feverish but content. He wraps himself around me and buries his face in my yellow kimono.

"Yes," he says.

Riku is different than I thought he would be but I love him more every day we spend together. He appears bold but is quite shy and easily startled. I know he had a brutal life in the mountains but he is a gentle soul, never harsh with me. Sometimes he is aggressive but only when he worries about my safety. Remembering his ferocity in his wolf form I smile to myself looking at him curl around me as I sing.

***

It's the middle of the night and I'm running. Riku does it. I can do it, too. Now that I'm a demon I'm not scared anymore. I tie the hem of my kimono short and put my hair up, exposing my neck. I take a scarlet berry and pinch it in between my fingers and paint my lips. I do all the things I know annoy him but they make me happy.

I'm sprinting through the forest, weaving around the evergreens and falling leaves. The spirits of the forest peek at me from boulders and ferns. I think they find me unusual. My hair sways and tickles my shoulder. I let out a laugh even though no one is around. I feel so free.

I don't mean to worry Riku or Hanako but I find solace in my own company from time to time. They still treat me as though I were human but I can take care of myself now. The wind picks up and it's raining red and yellow. I dance to music that's not there but I hear it in my heart. Catching a gold leaf in my palm I think of Riku's eyes. I long to see them.

"Hey there," a syrupy voice calls to me from the cedars. I look to see a man with dark wavy hair and black ears. Another jaguar demon.

"Hi," I say.

I stop dancing and study the man. He has sapphire eyes like the tiger demon. His light skin is flawless as it moves over the muscles in his arms. The jaguar wears blue trousers and nothing else.

"I've been watching you. You're the most beautiful woman I have ever seen."

The jaguar hangs from the branch in the tree with his legs, his spotted tail swishing back and forth.

"Thank you..." I didn't plan on talking to anyone.

This was supposed to be my time alone. The man jumps out of the tree and lands on his feet with grace. As he closes the gap I see he is quite tall, almost as tall as Riku. He reaches for my face but I hiss at him and recoil. This makes him laugh.

"I like them feisty," he says. The jaguar aims to grab me but I put my fist up and call upon the flames.

"Don't touch me!" I snap.

"You're a woman of fire. I see now. How peculiar," he hums his words in his wildcat throat.

"What do you mean?" I ask.

"You are a fire demon but you don't reek of toxicity or sulfur. The blood in your veins is red."

"I guess I'm special," I mutter.

"You are. I can tell," he says.

"Is that so?" I'm growing annoyed with the perverted cat.

"Yes. I see everything in this part of the forest. I've been alive for six centuries, I've never met a fire demon that didn't have darkness in their heart."

"Now you've seen it all," I spit. He chuckles again. Cats have a roar to their laughter.

"Yes, I have. Take care, fire girl," says the jaguar.

With no more left to say, he jumps into the high branches and vanishes into the canopy. I never thought about that. Kasai made me in his image, a fire demon. Somehow I was able to take control of my mind and prevent my blood from running black and poisonous.

It's almost dawn. I should get back to Riku and Hanako. Hanako tends to get up early but Riku sleeps in. I hope he doesn't notice I'm gone. He gets cross with me but I don't mind.

We aren't the type to fight and are over our quarrels rather quickly. The sun is a sliver in the east giving the hillside a halo. I stop to breathe it all in. Pink and yellow butterflies hover above me. I reach out to them. One lands on my ring finger and stays there. She has jade eyes and long pretty black legs.

"Aiya!" Riku calls my name and she flies away. My smile fades as soon as I look up. "Aiya! Where have you been? I've been looking for you all night."

Riku is much more cross than I anticipated.

"I'm sorry. I just wanted to be by myself. You do it, too."

"That's different." He takes my hand and we begin walking back to where Hanako is.

"How?" I ask

"It just is," he says.

His voice is gruff but his touch is gentle. I don't want to argue so I keep my mouth shut. Hanako is still sleeping. Her red and black ears twitch as does her nose. Riku sits down against a tree and I lay in his lap. He seems bothered by this gesture but I want to watch the sunrise with him. I turn my gaze to the sliver of gold as it manifests into a full circle and catch Riku eyeing my neck and scarlet lips. I'm pretending not to notice when I feel my hair cascade over my shoulder. Riku is holding my hair ribbon.

"I love you," I say and kiss him. The scent of wild berries tints the air between us. He brushes the locks of hair out of my face.

"I love you."

He doesn't seem as mad anymore. The birds start to sing signifying the beginning of another beautiful day. Riku is touching my bottom lip, "Why do you do this?" I know he is talking about the red stain.

"It makes me feel pretty."

"You are pretty," he says. Riku is staring at my berry mouth and collar bone.

"You think so?" I put my arms around him and he holds me a little tighter.

"Yes."

CHAPTER THIRTEEN

Anything for You

Winter is here and snowflakes stick in my hair. I fan it out as I spin and catch icy kisses on my tongue. I snuck away again but only for a little bit. With the last of my human money I had a woman in a small village nearby make me a red kimono. It has gold and black flowers on it. A present to myself. I tie it short so I can run. My feet are never cold, they melt the snow as I race through the evergreens.

I throw up my arms and embrace the chilly embrace from the heavens. Everything is beautiful this time of year. I love the beginning of winter. I am a drop of ruby ink on paper. This time of year the winterberries are more pink than red. I squeeze one in between my slender fingers and paint my lips. I tie my hair up and pull two pieces down to frame my face. The cold has made my cheeks rosy, accentuating my freckles.

Smiling to myself I skip on the frozen ground but remain untouched by the frost. There is a song in my heart and I'm singing to myself with my eyes closed. My eyelashes tickle my cheeks. I'm having so much fun I don't notice the cat and it's too late. I look over my shoulder to see the jaguar demon with emerald eyes has pounced on me.

"Get off of me," I shout. I thrash but he is too heavy to move.

"You're even prettier when you fight me," he purrs. I hiss at him and bare my fangs. He seems to enjoy it so I stop.

"Don't touch me. Get off of me!" I scream. No matter how much I flail I can't get away.

"If you didn't want me to touch you then why are you running around the forest looking like this." He's touching my thighs and pushing up my kimono.

"Stop! No," I try to call on the flames but I can't. I'm too distracted by the jaguar demon pressing into me, "Let me go! Stop!" I don't mean to but I start to cry. The man is laughing in my ear.

"I like it better when they cry."

He kisses me on the lips. His rough tongue is in my mouth. I thrash again but he pins me down. There is a massive hand in my kimono touching my breasts and my stomach. He licks my neck and purrs in my ear. It vibrates in his throat touching my shoulder.

"Please! Stop—"

I try to call on the flames again but there is nothing. Unable to focus, I continue to writhe. I'm panicking as the cat rips off my new kimono. It lays in the snow looking lonely, like it was worn by a ghost that has vanished without a trace. Now the cat is pulling on my hair and sniffing me. His skin is hot but I am freezing cold.

"Don't! Please, no. Stop—You're hurting me," I shriek.

"Begging isn't doing you any favors," he purrs.

All of a sudden the weight of the jaguar demon is gone and I hear a loud growl to my left. It's Riku. He's on top of the jaguar demon.

"Riku!" I reach out to him but he doesn't hear me.

He's too busy sinking his jaws into the man's throat. The jaguar yowls and his emerald eyes go wide. The animalistic sound of cats and dogs fighting rumbles the forest floor, knocking snow out of the trees.

The man scratches Riku across the face with his sharp claws but he doesn't even flinch. Riku begins ripping out the jaguar demon's vocal cords, shredding the muscle, and spitting out tiny bones. He headbutts the jaguar and blood pours out of his ears. I watch in horror as the love of my life murders someone in front of me without a second thought.

Even though the man was going to violate me I don't want to see him die. I thought Riku would stop but he grows more violent, pulling the cat's hair this way and that to shred both sides of his neck. There is blood all over his face and shoulders.

As his jaws re-enter the man's flesh crimson ink sprays across the armor he wears. The liquid makes a sloppy hollow sound against the steel. He keeps spitting out pieces of the man and growling. The cat attempts to fight him but is dead in a matter of minutes. I can't move and sit naked in the snow, clutching the kimono I just bought.

Once the paper white snow is drenched in red Riku stops. He coughs up the last of the wildcat's blood and wipes his face with the back of his hand. I'm shivering but not because of the cold. Riku kneels down next to me. I am in a daze as I stare at the body of the jaguar demon. His eyes are glossy. The rest of his face is unidentifiable as is his neck. Riku tore apart everything above the cat demon's shoulders.

"Are you okay?" he asks. I nod but I don't think I'm really okay.

Riku takes off his cloak and covers me up. He picks me up and starts carrying me. I want to protest but I can't talk or walk. For some reason I am chilled to the bone. I know I should be grateful but I feel torn. The jaguar demon was despicable. He was going to ruin me. Yet the brutal death he experienced seemed excessive. I am new to this world. Its rules, their laws, they are different from humanity's. Perhaps I am just naive.

"Why did you do that?" I whisper. I didn't mean to ask but the words escape my berry stained lips. Riku looks perplexed by my question and stops walking to look at me.

"I did it for you," he says.

His answer is sincere and it brings down the wall growing in front of my heart. I kiss him, even though his face is smeared with the cat demon's blood. It smells metallic and musky. The red liquid drips from his chin and he spits more out, staining the white below.

"Thank you."

I'm genuine but still confused by my feelings. Why does my scorching hot blood run cool and my spine tingle? It's because this is the first time I've seen Riku as a killer.

***

I wait until Riku goes off by himself to tell Hanako about the jaguar demon. Her ears turn downward and she covers her magnolia lips with her delicate hands in shock. She waits patiently for me to cry through the story. It moves through me like a storm and I can't help but convulse as the rain falls from my face. Hanako embraces me and strokes my hair to try and make me feel better.

"Hanako, do you think Riku is dangerous?" I sob.

"No, Aiya. Of course not. Riku was protecting you the only way he knows how. I know he scared you but he would never hurt you," she whispers.

"I don't worry about him hurting me. I am afraid of what will happen to other people," my confession is sand and embers in my mouth.

The words are bitter and I choke on them. Hanako pulls away to look at me. She studies my sad face and wipes away my tears. Her short eyelashes and round nose gives her a childlike appearance but she is clever. The most clever person I know.

"The jaguar demon was going to ruin you," she says with no inflection.

"Do you think what Riku did to him was okay?" Hanako's ears twitch at my question and she looks down to think about it.

"I would rather you keep your virtue and the jaguar be dead than for him to have it and be alive. I think Riku feels the same way." My friend surprises me. Perhaps demon laws will make more sense to me in the future.

"Thank you, Hanako." It hurts but I smile. She takes my hands in hers.

"He would do anything for you. Kill, steal, destroy. I know it must frighten you but he has a good heart. Remember that, okay?"

"I'll remember," I say.

"You promise?" she asks.

"I promise."

***

I'm skipping around, twirling in the snow. It's raining down from the heavens and I love the way it feels on my burning skin. For the past two weeks I've felt feverish but not ill. I'm so happy I am beyond myself. It feels like a dream but it isn't. I pinch myself to make sure. I put my hair up but Riku keeps taking out my hair ribbon.

Everything he does endears him closer to me. The way he looks for me as I hide in the cedars, how he says my name, the quiet way he cares. It is all magnificent to me. There is no detail about him that goes unnoticed. I see how he can sit next to me and disappear inside himself. Riku can be in one hundred places at once.

I know he loves me though. It's the small gestures that he isn't aware of. It makes my heart flutter when he takes out my hair ribbon, letting me know he wants it down. I catch him watching me all the time. He holds me too tight but I don't mind. It makes me feel safe. Standing with Riku is standing with an army and I will never be afraid again.

My kimono is short but he doesn't try to untie it. I'm not very tall but my legs are long and I dance like a winter crane. The berries are bright scarlet and I tint my lips. Riku and I have been talking about favorites and I'm excited to learn everything about him. We're laughing about how disgusting he finds spicy food when I hear Hanako's voice behind me.

"Hey guys!" she exclaims. I run to embrace her and she swings me in a full circle. My hair covers us like an inky cloak. She has a bundle on her back.

"Hello Hanako. What's going on?" asks Riku.

"I received a message. My father would like to see me. I'm going back home for the winter. I haven't seen him in three years. I miss him," she says. Now I'm worried.

"Is something wrong?" I ask.

"No, everything is fine. It's just time for me to return to the western fox tribe." Hanako brushes the hair from my face. Snow sticks to her red ears and sparkly hair. She is iridescent.

"I'll miss you," I whisper.

"Don't worry, I'll never abandon you. Winter won't be forever. Where do you guys want me to meet you in the spring?" asks Hanako. I know exactly where I want to go.

"Meet us at my village."

"Okay! I'll see you two when the cherry blossoms start to bloom. Take care," she says as she hugs me and then Riku. It's cute to see the way it warms his heart to have a friend like her. She whispers something to him but I don't catch it. I'll let it be their secret, "Goodbye, Aiya! Bye, Riku!"

"Goodbye, Hanako! Don't forget me," I say.

"I could never forget you," she says as she vanishes into the white abyss.

I realize this is the first time Riku and I have truly been alone as a couple. It's exciting but I'm nervous.

"Where do you want to go?" he asks me. I know where I want to go but I think about it for a moment.

"I've been having so much fun here with you. But I kind of miss my home as well. Would you mind if we spent the winter there? I haven't visited Chiyo."

"I will go anywhere you want to go," he says.

***

Since it's been just us I have asked Riku countless questions. I worry I am bothering him but he answers them all without showing annoyance. Hungry to know everything about him and wanting him to understand me, I talk more than I ever have. I'm not shy about my affection for him anymore. We walk hand in hand and kiss constantly. I hide in the cedars and pounce on him throughout the day.

"Riku! Look!"

I see a hot spring surrounded by winter peonies. They are pink like Hanako's mouth. I gather a couple flower heads, stems, and their leaves. Taking off my kimono I peek over my shoulder to see if Riku is looking at me. His gaze somewhere else. I wade into the clear water with the steam swirling around my thighs.

Taking a deep breath I hide at the bottom. It's peaceful and quiet under the water. I could stay down here forever. Bubbles rise to the surface slowly from my mouth. Wondering what it's like to be a ghost I look up to see a gray and white sky lined with cedar branches. I break the surface and throw back my hair and let it stick to my body. "Are you going to join me?" I ask. I expect him to say "no" but he does. The pile of peonies turns into a paste as I crush it with a small rock.

"What are you doing?" he asks.

I take the floral potion and rub it in his snowy locks.

"Lady Kiyori taught me about useful properties in certain plants. This will make your hair soft and smell good."

I coat my hair, a veil of black, with the rest of the peony paste. It smells sweet and creamy. I look over to see Riku glance at me but not turn his head. He is an honorable person but it makes me giggle. I've told him he can look at me but he refuses.

"What's so funny?" he asks.

"Nothing."

"Please. Tell me."

"It's just that I didn't expect you to be so..." I trail off. I don't want to offend him.

"So what?" he asks.

"So pure," I say.

"Is that a bad thing?"

"No, of course not."

I push back from the rocky edge and vanish into the middle of the hot spring. The heat is soothing. My hair floats around me, I pull my fingers through it to feel the silky blackness.

The floral potion tints the water pink. It looks like magic. I watch it swirl, the bubbles break, and holes form in the magic ribbons. I hear Riku calling my name and I sneak up to squirt water in his face hoping to make him smile. He seems cross. I don't want him to yell at me.

"I'm sorry, Riku."

"It's okay," he says.

His face changes as he speaks with his quiet but rough voice. Anything he says is music to me. I'm happy when he shares what's on his mind. I still talk more but he has opened up since we've been alone. He puts his arms around me and I listen to his heartbeat. It is measured and even. Mine beats light and fast. I look up at his handsome face and grab his shoulders. Pulling him into the water with me I kiss him for a very long time.

The heat of the hot spring is familiar like a home, or a womb. Riku pulls away from me and breaks the surface, coughing up water. There's something striking and attractive about Riku's face when he looks surprised. I don't mean to but I laugh again. It must drive Riku mad.

I get out of the hot spring and try to contain myself as I wring out the water from my hair. The black ink is a veil covering most of my figure but I see Riku peek at me. It lights a fire inside and I find myself overwhelmed by my feelings. To hide my feverish face I skip down the path in front of Riku but hear no footsteps. I look over my shoulder at him to see he hasn't moved.

"I'll be there in a minute. Go ahead without me," he says.

I'm confused but I do as he asks and skip through the frozen ground, melting everything in my wake.

***

Every day I ask Riku more questions. I learn as much as I can. My need to know him is insatiable. His favorite color is green, his favorite food is salmon, he likes baby blue bells, his fiance married his older brother, he misses his sisters Yama and Yuri, our favorite time of year is winter. We appreciate the stillness and the silence. It's beautiful.

Riku talks more and I enjoy hearing him express himself. He used to say he liked whatever I liked but I am persistent in his individuality. I want to know the things that make him happy, what does he think about, where does he go as I lay in his arms and feel him disappear? I love him but it's exhausting trying to hold on to him. It's like loving a ghost.

I asked him why he didn't come back for me. To my relief he did but he didn't approach me. I think I know the day, it was my sixteenth birthday. There was the snap of a twig breaking and I felt as though I was being watched. I peered into the shadowy forest but couldn't see anyone. At the time I was too afraid to take a single step into the dark woods.

I don't want to talk about it too much because he gets tense so I skip ahead of him as we approach my village. Out of the corner of my eye I glance at the hill where the white flowers grow, the place of my transformation. Kasai violated me but he also gave me a precious gift. The ability to live with Riku forever is worth more than all the silver and gold in the world. The fire demon may have made me in his image but I can choose who I am. I choose to be Aiya. Brother Minoru told me being touched by darkness doesn't mean we must succumb to darkness. I try to live by those words.

We are greeted by Natsume, Hiromi, and Daina. Their shrill voices are startling but familiar. It's good to be home. Riku and I walk through the village hand in hand. Not many people are out. Three priestesses pass us. One of them has light gold hair and green eyes. I've never seen anyone with sunny hair like hers. Riku looks at her a second longer than the other priestesses. I wonder who she reminds him of.

I'm excited to be back at my house. Living freely in the forest was fun but I long to sleep in my bed and be surrounded by my items. I miss my teapot, the fragrant floral powders and oils I would wear, my comb and mirror. I yearn to feel the softness of my blankets and pillows. My kimonos are bright reds, yellows, and blues. I love them. I am fire in red, the storm in blue, and summer in yellow. Riku refused to come into my home when we first met but he walks in without any protest behind me.

I start the fire with my hand. It takes me no time at all now. We are never cold. Riku makes himself comfortable. He removes his armor and I fix the collar of his shirt. I touch his shoulders that are never without the heavy metal. It's nice to see him like this.

"I'll be right back. Wait here." I go to Hiromi's house. Daina is here but the husbands are gone. They look me up and down and smile wide grins. Their thick eyelids cover their dark eyes causing them to appear sleepy but content.

"Aiya! What are you doing here?" asks Hiromi.

"I wanted to visit. Also I was wondering if you could do me a favor." I step in and the ladies begin playing with my hair. They fawn over me the way a mother would even though they are only a few years older than me.

"What is it?" asks Hiromi with a pleased face.

She loves doing things for the neighbors. A friendly and helpful soul. Daina enjoys growing herbs to dry and give as gifts. They are like Chiyo, sweet and willing to put in the effort for the ones they love.

"Could you make me and Riku some of those amazing salmon rice balls? I could do you a favor. Perhaps wash your husband's filthy laundry," I joke and the ladies cackle the way I imagine witches do.

"No, no. I would love to! It would be my pleasure. No need to touch his disgusting clothes," teases Hiromi as she starts preparing the rice.

"Aiya, you are too kind! If you washed it you would probably faint and fall into the river," laughs Daina. Hiromi hits her arm but in a playful way.

"Are you sure? I would hate to be a bother," I start but Hiromi cuts me off.

"No, you and Riku saved us. I could never ask you to do me a favor. Please, let me do this for you," says Hiromi. Her voice is low this time. Daina nods to agree.

"Okay, if you insist. If you ever need anything, just ask. I would do anything to help," I offer. The ladies look to each other and smile. They speak using their eyes that pierce the other's mind.

"How are you and Riku? He seems happy," says Daina in a sugary voice.

"We are still getting acquainted but we spend our days happy. We are lucky to have so much time to get to know each other," I say.

"He is a good man. Selfless and kind," says Hiromi with confidence.

"Yes. We are glad to have him in our lives. Thank you, Aiya," says Daina. There is a silence where we stare into the fire and our smiles grow like wildflowers.

"They're ready! Here you go." Hiromi hands me a tray of delicious fare.

"These are beautiful. Thank you!" I say.

"Tell Riku I wanted to make them, okay? He needs to know he is appreciated," says Hiromi.

"Yes. We owe him our lives. You too, Aiya. We're so glad you're back. Welcome home," says Daina as she hugs me with her chubby arms. She smells like lilacs.

"I'll tell him. Thank you. Have a good night." I slip out the door and return to my love with our treats. It's the most precious scene. I find Riku in my bed.

"I told Hiromi your favorite food is salmon and she made you these."

"Thank you. She didn't have to do that." Everything he says makes my blood effervescent. I feel it tinting my cheeks pink.

"She said she wanted to."

"Are you happy to be home?" he asks.

"I'm always happy now," I say.

We share a meal in my home for the first time. I can tell he's tired and motion for him to lay down. He falls asleep almost in an instant. I pull the blanket over his shoulders. The rise and fall of his chest is slow and steady. Eating the rest of my dinner I watch him smile in his sleep. He must be so tired from all my games and chasing me around. I tell myself to stop running him ragged. Riku is strong but he needs me to take care of him, too.

I stay up a little longer to look at my belongings and smell my floral citrus oil. I comb my long black hair and trace the freckles on my face. Riku loves them. I catch him staring at the stars and yearning to be near them. He acts as though I am out of reach but he is the one who won't let me in. I throw off my kimono and get into bed. He is a frozen lake and I warm him with the embers in my heart.

CHAPTER FOURTEEN

Wait for Me

I wake up and Riku is gone. Touching his side of the bed I feel it's still warm. Where did he go? I could go visit Chiyo but I can't concentrate on conversation. Laying on his side I inhale the pine and ice. After I can no longer rest I get up and throw on my blue kimono. Stepping outside I admire the falling snow and let it kiss my face.

Not wanting to feel guilty, I tell myself we will visit Chiyo tomorrow. I can't leave until he comes back to me. Waiting for him is my favorite pastime. I pick white daffodils and pluck their petals. A trail of stems and leaves are scattered everywhere I go. Pacing around my house in the snow has me spinning and singing to myself.

The forest I have roamed
So happy to be home
The wolf is mine
He will never be alone

I don't mind spending some time by myself. It is a rarity for me these days. Not that I want to be alone but I do enjoy the solace of my own company. The sun is beginning to set. The orange sky makes the snow glow and the shadows are black ink spilling across the hills. I wish Riku was here to see this with me. When the last of the yellow orb drops below the horizon I go back in the house. Unable to relax, I lean in the doorway. Like a beautiful illusion I see him walking towards me.

"Riku! I was worried about you. Where did you go?" I ask.

"Lady Kiyori and Brother Minoru needed my help," he says.

Riku is carrying his armor. It is drenched in blood. His shoulder is wrapped in a thick bandage. Red ink bleeds through in some spots. His left hand is also injured. I pull him inside and have him sit with me.

"What happened?"

"There was a small army of boar demons. I was able to kill them by myself. I didn't want anybody to get hurt," he says.

Riku's gruff voice is strained from pain. I don't want to bother him but I need to touch him. Cautious of the wounds I put my arms around his neck.

"Are you okay?" I look up at his face–it's perfect but perpetually mysterious.

"I'm fine, Aiya. I promise." He always says he's fine. I know he can't be fine all the time.

"Thank you for protecting my family," I say.

"I would do anything for you," he whispers.

I don't know what to say. He has done so much for me. I kiss him as I always do when I am without words. It's early but he falls asleep. I watch as he winces in pain and the red spots on the bandage get bigger. It's selfish of me but I sneak out of the house and into the dark forest. I want to practice calling on the flames.

At first there is nothing. The more I focus the more I feel a warmth build up in my lungs and my arms. This time I am successful and a small fire sits in the palm of my hand but does not burn me. I am in awe of my own magic.

"Cool trick," says a husky female voice.

I turn around to see a woman with curly red hair growing past her waist. Her sly and narrow eyes are mossy green. As she approaches I see she has a long red tail that's fluffy at the end and thinner at the base. She wears a jade kimono accenting her eyes. Curly copper hair hangs in her face but I can still see she's pretty. Well defined eyebrows with cherry lips. I sense she is not a threat.

"Thank you." I put the flames out.

"You're beautiful," she says.

"So are you," I say. She smiles at this. Her canines are long and sharp like mine and Riku's.

"Thanks. You're a woman of fire but you don't smell of rot. How is that so?" she asks with curious green eyes.

"I'm special," is all I think to say.

"Special, huh? I like that. My name is Bara."

"My name is Aiya."

"I think I like Special better. You should be careful out here. The monkey demons have been invading this part of the forest. Real creeps, if you know what I mean."

She flips her long hair over her shoulder and pushes her bangs out of her face. Now I see she has freckles, too.

"Call me whatever you like. If I may ask, what are you?" I ask.

"I'm a red coyote." She answers without contempt.

"I've never met a red coyote."

"There aren't many of us. We used to travel in packs but a lot of us split from the group."

"Why?"

"I'm not sure why. I just knew I wanted something different than everybody else," she says.

"I understand." I nod and think about her words. They resonate with me.

"Well, I gotta get going. Nice to meet you, Special. See ya around." With that she scampers off beyond the camphors and oak trees. I decide to go home. No monkey demons stop me but I am wary of the beasts lurking in the dark. I get home and slip into bed. Riku's sleep is still fitful but he relaxes in my arms. I kiss his neck and sing to him even though he can't hear me.

***

I get up at dawn and take Riku's clothes to the river. They are soaked in blood. There is a tear in the right shoulder of the black bodysuit. I'll sew it later. As I scrub out the red ink crimson clouds float downstream. I hear a familiar voice across the way.

"I didn't take you for the kind of woman to do her man's dirty laundry," says Bara. She emerges from the ferns and sits down in front of me.

"I didn't use to be," I laugh.

"I smell his blood. Is he okay?" she asks. Her narrow but pretty green eyes look at me with empathy.

"He's injured but okay. My lover is strong. He was able to fight an army of boar demons and protect my village." I continue washing out the blood. There are sheer red stains on my fingers.

"What's his name?" Bara takes a handful of water and runs it through her copper locks, lively like fire.

"His name is Riku," I say.

"Is he a wolf demon?" Her question causes me to stop what I'm doing.

"Yes."

"The disgraced wolf prince from the north. I have heard stories of him." Bara turns up the corners of her cherry mouth.

"What have you heard?" I ask with intense curiosity.

"That he is noble and kind. Protector of the people. He is special, like you." The red coyote wags her tail and smiles at me.

"Thank you. He is indescribable. More precious than words could say," I whisper into his undershirt. It has bright scarlet splotches.

"I'm happy he has someone like you," says Bara. She takes another scoop of water and cleans her teeth.

"What makes you say that?" I continue my work. I still need to stop by Lady Kiyori's.

"I've seen him several times over the years. Always alone. He is incredibly handsome but his eyes were quite forlorn. I am sure he smiles often now." Bara winks at me.

"Yes. He smiles every day." I wring out the freezing water from his clothes.

"Good. You love him so much it hurts. I can tell. Don't let it deter you. The best things in life are complicated," she says.

The red coyote gets up and rustles the hydrangeas as she runs off. I'm confused but content. I head to the priestess's home. Standing outside I feel nervous. I ignore it and knock on her door.

"Aiya! It's good to see you." She embraces me and touches my cheek with care.

"It's good to be back, Lady Kiyori." I smile with warmth.

"Is Riku okay?" She ushers me inside and hands me a cup of tea.

"He's okay but his bandage is soaked through. Could you give me some new ones, please?" I ask.

"Of course. I will give you some herbal powder to prevent infection as well," she says. Lady Kiyori gets a basket and begins gathering the medical supplies for me.

"Thank you."

"Take him these. They will help him heal faster," she says and places a bowl of steamy lotus roots along with the other items.

"Yes. I'll be sure to take good care of him." I accept the basket and she holds my hand for a moment.

"I know you will. Riku is part of our family. Make sure he knows that." Lady Kiyori looks at me with her serious gaze holding intelligence and compassion. Dark bangs frame her face. We both have the same tiny nose and thin rosy mouth. She could have been my mother's sister.

"I try but he remains distant from me," I admit. I didn't mean to say the words out loud.

"He will come around. Give him time."

She lets me go. I make my way down the path to my house. The sun hasn't been up for very long. I hope he didn't wake up and worry about me.

"Riku?" I open the door. He tries to sit up and greet me but grabs his shoulder in pain.

"Hey," his voice is quieter than usual and hoarse.

"Don't move so fast," I say and sit down next to him.

With gentle hands I remove the blood soaked bandage. There's so much blood. I want to cry but I keep a straight face. I pour hot water into a bowl and mix in the herbal concoction Lady Kiyori gave me.

Towel after towel I clean the enormous wound starting at the top of his shoulder and ends above his elbow. His hip and lower ribs are badly bruised as well. Purple and green stain his fair skin. The sacrifices he makes for me will tear my heart apart. I gingerly secure the new bandage. This one is thicker.

"Thank you," he says.

"You don't have to thank me."

The herbal water smells like pine needles and camphor. It's refreshing but overpowering. Riku doesn't complain though. Next I clean his hand.

The boar demon's blood has caused tiny blisters and burns to his palm and the top of his wrist. He grits his teeth and I can tell he wants to say something but he doesn't. As fast as I can I remove the bloody towel and cover the wound in a soft bandage.

"It feels much better," he says.

"I brought you breakfast and washed your clothes," I say.

"Thanks." His voice is tight in his throat. He's in a mood. I should leave him be.

"I'm going out for a little bit. I'll check on you soon, okay?" I kiss him like a ghost and dart out the door. I don't want to argue. In the forest I hide and practice calling on the flames. It's getting easier with each day.

I check on Riku, he's sleeping as expected. He's eaten the food I brought him and drank the water I left. I light the fire and head back into the woods until it's dark. Then I go to Chiyo's house.

"Aiya! It's so good to see you!" Chiyo squeezes me.

"I missed you," I squeak. My best friend strokes my hair and eyes me up and down.

"You look amazing," she sighs.

Haru comes up behind her. She is sixteen, the same age I was when I fell in love with Riku. Her hair is unique. It's brown but has streaks of copper and gold. On the left side of her cheek is a dimple. It's accented by her bright pouty lips. It's no wonder Yuta didn't have the courage to profess his love. She is entrancing to look at.

"Hi Aiya! Where's Riku?" asks Haru. She's twirling her rainbow hair and blushing.

"He's at my house. Would you like to see him? I ask.

"Yes!" Both of them shriek. I hope Riku is up for company. We enter my house. He's awake.

"Hey, Riku. How are you feeling?" asks Chiyo. She is the first one in.

"Hi, Chiyo. I'm okay," he says.

"Thank you for protecting us, Riku," says Haru.

"You're welcome." Riku sounds out of breath.

"Do you need anything?" I ask. I rub the back of his neck but not too hard.

"No, I'm fine." Riku closes his eyes as we make small talk.

"I'm really happy to see you two. You seem very in love. It's so sweet," says Chiyo. She looks down at Riku and back up at me with her shiny dark blue eyes like morning glory blossoms.

"It's good to be home," I say.

As the words leave my mouth Haru moves across the floor. Her pink kimono rustles as she kneels next to Riku. I can tell she is fascinated by him.

"Can I touch your hair?" she asks. Riku looks at me for permission and I nod my head. I think Haru's infatuation with the wolf demon is endearing. Her youthful face stares at him in wonder as she lifts up his bangs. Haru has chestnut eyes like Hanako. "Wow," she gasps.

"What?" asks Riku.

"You are flawless. I've never seen someone as gorgeous as you," says Haru.

Riku appears shy and hides his face. Chiyo and I try to be polite but a giggle escapes her berry mouth. I manage to keep mine in.

"Thank you," he mumbles. I see him look at Haru for a moment, studying her with his amber eyes. "Your hair is very beautiful. I've never seen anything like it."

His compliment causes Haru to blush. She bites her lip and smiles to herself.

"Really?" she asks.

"Yes, I swear." he answers.

"Thank you." I think the wolf prince has put the young girl under a spell.

"Oh, before I forget!" exclaims Chiyo.

She disappears but returns with two large bowls. "I made you two dinner. It's rice porridge with salmon." My best friend smiles at Riku to show him she cares.

"You didn't have to do that, Chiyo. Thank you," he says.

"I wanted to. It brings me joy to cook for the people I love. You two need your rest. Enjoy your dinner. I'll see you tomorrow! Goodnight!" Chiyo and Haru go back home and we are alone.

"I missed you today. Did you miss me?" I ask.

Examining the bandage I see no red splotches. I get into bed and Riku places his hand on my hip. His movements are slow and sleepy. The wound must ache and make his rest unsatisfying. The hand he holds me with is heavy but the weight relaxes me. It is an anchor and I am the sea.

"I always miss you," he says.

"I never want to be without you."

"You won't be. I'm right here."

Riku kisses me before fading out. I miss him even though he's in my bed. Putting my ear to his heart I try to hear the story he won't tell me.

CHAPTER FIFTEEN

Captured By Fate

My hand finds him missing. It's cold on his side of the bed and I feel dejected. This time I don't lay around and sulk. I put on my yellow kimono, his favorite one. I tie it shorter than usual. Walking up a trail into the forest I find the reddest berry I can find and paint my lips. I tie up my hair and expose my collarbone. The ground is frozen beneath the snow but I am burning up. I weave through the forest. Who is it I'm racing? Am I running away? Perhaps I am being pulled towards something.

I spend most of the day like this. Half wanting to be caught I pick white daffodils and put them in my hair. I sing his favorite songs. There is something tugging at the strings in my heart. Does Riku love me the way I love him? We are lovers but strangers. He is my hero but he says he is the lucky one. The one I love says he loves me back but I'm afraid it won't last forever. Am I cursed again? Is this fate or disaster?

My racing thoughts are a constricting snake. The palpitations in my heart leave me feeling bitter. I keep up like this until I see the massive footprints in the snow. They aren't meant for a beast, not human either though. I remember what Hanako said the monkey demons did to her siblings. How they ripped off her mother's head. The vile beasts killed her whole family. I'm happy she has her father. Bara warned me of the terrible creatures but in my selfishness I've wandered further than usual. A twig snaps and my blood halts in my veins.

"Well, well, well." It's a giant monkey demon. He wears purple trousers and a red vest. His baton is gold and embellished with multicolored jewels. His face is flat with a wide nose but still resembles a person. The tail is long and white. He wears his straight white hair up and adorned with gold hair pins.

"Get away from me," I hiss. He licks his lips at me. They're fat and purple like his trousers.

"Why would I do that? Not only are you pretty as can be but you smell nice, too! Floral with a hint of honey," he laughs.

"Don't."

"Come here, beautiful. I can show you a good time!" The man lunges at me.

"Leave me alone!" I call on the flames. The monkey demon's eyes widen.

"You're a woman of fire," he gasps.

His massive foot takes another step and I put up the barrier. I hear him calling to me but I ignore it. Waiting an extra long time to make sure he's gone it's dark when I decide to put down the wall of flames. My heart is pounding in my chest. I'm frightened and rush home. Riku is asleep. I light the fire and crawl into bed. A shiver runs from the tips of my toes to the top of my head. Feeling needy and afraid I wrap my arms and legs around him. He makes me feel safe. My army, my hero.

Drifting away I am in and out of a light slumber. There are no nightmares but I hear the monkey demon's words echo in my mind. I roll onto my side but the man's voice won't leave me be. Laying on my back I look at the ceiling and see the jaguar's emerald green eyes.

Grimacing at the memory I turn to look at my lover. Riku is having a peaceful sleep. His breaths are light and airy. I want to be close and kiss his neck. Knowing I should stop slows me down but I don't. I grip his collar with a needy fist.

"Please, don't." He's awake.

"Do you not like when I kiss you?" I'm hurt but try not to show it.

"I like it too much," he says. Riku smiles at me and starts to play with my hair. One of the many things he does that makes my heart swell and my sternum stings from keeping it in.

"We don't have to wait," I say. My words hang in the air.

"I want to wait," he says as he picks up my hair and folds it around his wrist.

"Why?" I ask. The word holds a thousand reasons but he gives me only one.

"I just do. Please, it's important to me."

Riku is stern with me. I nod my head to acknowledge I hear him. The wolf prince adheres to high standards and remains honorable.

"Whatever you want." I always let him win. Biting his bottom lip I imagine him succumbing to my desires. It's the last thing I think of as I fade into a deep sleep.

***

We spend most of the day with Chiyo, Haru, and Yuta. I can tell Riku is tired but he makes no mention of his exhaustion. I tell them we have to go and they wave goodbye with smiling faces. The night sky greets us with a shooting star. We both gasp.

"I love you," he says. I'm a bit surprised. He says it first all the time now.

"I love you." I kiss him and we keep walking, "Do you ever wish on the stars?" I ask.

"I don't have to. You are my girl, the one with stars on her face," he says. Riku is thoughtful with his words. They are never without meaning.

"I wished for us to be together forever."

"Don't worry. We will be." His words shock me again.

"You promise?" I ask.

"I promise."

"It's okay if one day you don't love me anymore. I won't be mad," I say. Riku grabs my wrist and stops us in the middle of the path.

"Why would you say that?" he asks. I worry he's going to scold me.

"It's just that I love you so much. I wouldn't want you to stay with me if you were unhappy," I shrug. I didn't realize what I said would upset him like this.

"I'll always love you. I should have come back for you sooner. Please, don't think I would ever stop loving you."

The wolf demon's plea makes my heart bleed. My ribcage fills up, reducing the air in my lungs. Maybe Riku really does love me after all.

"If you had one wish what would it be?"

"I'd wish to go back in time. The day I heard you sing about me. I'd go back and kiss you. Seeing you cry as you sang still haunts me." He keeps his head down. I don't want him to feel guilty.

"It's okay, Riku. I'm glad we met the way we did," I say.

"You are?" He perks up at my words.

"Yes. My journey to find you taught me a lot. I learned to believe in myself and have faith in you. You heard me call your name and you came running. I think that's when we were destined to meet again."

"I think so, too." His voice is soft. We get into bed and I look into his eyes, gold and sad.

"Riku, can I ask you a question?"

"What is it?" he asks.

"You told me about your brother Ryo and your sisters Yuri and Yama. Do you have any other siblings?" I can't help but steal a few more answers.

"Yes. My sister Rena is the eldest and most vicious. She should have been queen but my father was against the idea of a female leader. My little brother Yahei betrayed me after I fled the challenge. He let Ryo manipulate him after he became king," he says.

"What makes everyone so ruthless?"

"It's the demonic canon. Wolf demons follow the word of an ancient book. Our religion asks us to destroy and take. It wants us to subdue others with our strength. War is a necessity because of our greed and need to rule. There is never enough gold, silk, or power." His upbringing is strange but the tales of his past engross me.

"You're not a believer?"

"No. I never believed that the king was a god."

"What do you know about the wolf god?" I wait patiently for his answer. When I look at the moon I wonder if he watches me. Is he the one who holds Riku captive? Can my love travel to the stars and back?

"Very little. My sister Yama was our spiritual leader. It's vague but her teachings said the wolf god was angered by humanity's increasing disrespect towards the forest. I was told he retreated into the spectral plain where he rules the mountains from beyond the moon," he says.

"Do the gods speak to you?" I ask.

"I spoke to a demigod. His name was Satoru."

"What did he say?" I am bubbling with excitement.

"He said you and I would be together for centuries." Riku is genuine. I can't believe what he's telling me.

"Did he really?" I ask with wide eyes.

"Yes, really. The gods' messenger brought me to you. I found your village because a white deer led me there," he says.

I've never been told any of this. There is more to mine and Riku's fate than I thought. It's faint but a memory comes to mind. I share it with him.

"I had a dream about a white deer once. The night before my sixteenth birthday. I saw it in the treeline next to the camphors and hydrangeas. There was someone in the forest with it but I couldn't see who it was. That morning I paced by the oaks and camphors outside the village for hours. I heard a twig snap and I thought someone was watching me."

"That was me," he admits. I knew it.

"You were just out of my reach." I touch his sculpted face.

"I'm sorry," he says.

"Don't be. I like our love story just the way it is." I love it even more now.

***

My best friend is in love but won't tell me who it is. She says she's not ready yet. I let her be. I know what it's like to not want to talk. Chiyo and I are at the hill where Kasai changed me. White daffodils and blue roses grow along the treeline. I find the baby rose bush filled with flowers. The day Riku came back, the day he heard me sing about him. I'm kind of glad he didn't approach me. I like how things turned out.

"It's so nice to have you home, Aiya."

Chiyo is placing blue roses in her obi with delicate hands. She is wearing an orange kimono with pink and white designs. I make a flower crown out of the daffodils and tie my hem short. Chiyo eyes me but doesn't say anything. She picks a rose that's darker blue than the others and she winces. I see she's pricked herself on the thorns,"Ouch!" she shrieks.

"Chiyo, be careful. They're sharp." I take her soft palm in mine and massage it. My claws are long but I know how to maneuver them so as to not scratch anyone. Chiyo is fascinated by them the way I was by Hanako's pretty hands.

"Thank you. That helped," she says in her clear bell voice. I let her go and we keep walking.

"I missed you," I say.

"I missed you, too. It hasn't been the same without you. I think about you all the time."

Chiyo clutches her heart. Putting my arm on her shoulder comforts her but she still seems sad.

"Not a day goes by I don't think of you. I hope you know that."

My answer pleases my best friend and her berry lips shine as the corners turn up. Her high cheekbones are excellently contoured and flattering. She is an authentic and kind person. I feel lucky she found me, too.

"What was it like living in the forest?" she asks. Her curiosity eases the tension.

"It was exciting. I had a lot of fun. Hanako and Riku showed me how to live." I don't tell her about the jaguar. It would upset her too much. She would worry and then we would both be unhappy.

Remembering Riku on top of the cat, shredding him apart, horrifies me. It's a sickly skeleton, an unwanted shadow. The cat may have tried to hurt me again. I know everything Riku does for me is out of love. I ignore the red ink and musky scented memory.

"Where did the three of you go?"

"Everywhere. I went to my old home. There was nothing there but it gave me closure to see it," I say.

The sun is out but it's still snowing. I love rain and snow. They are little messages from the gods. There is something important in every snowflake, every drop. Chiyo holds out her hand and receives pieces of a story. My eyelashes are long, they tickle my eyebrows. They hold the snowflakes and I see in crystal rainbow vision.

"How are you and Riku doing? You two seem very happy," she says and hands me a tiny blue rose with no thorns. I think about her question. Riku and I are fated to be together forever but know little of the other.

"We are. We are still getting acquainted but we're glad to know each other." Chiyo has flowers all around her tucked into the peachy obi. She takes my hand.

"What was the song you sang that made him fall in love with you?"

My best friend's dreamy blue eyes bore into me. Chiyo has creamy pale skin and ink black hair. She keeps hers to her shoulders. It's straight and shiny. Her nose is a tiny accent in the middle of her face. She could be my sister.

Was it you, was it you
Who left me by the spring
There was a man
I know he saved me but
I see him only in my dreams
Who was he, who was he

"Wow," whispers Chiyo but I keep singing.

Was it you, was it you
Who left me by the spring
I know your face
But not your name
I've been wondering
Who was he, who was he

I'm done with my song. Chiyo's dainty jaw has dropped. Her night blue eyes scan my face for more details. What is she looking for? I can't read her.

"What is it, Chiyo?" I ask

"It's no wonder why he fell in love. Your voice is beautiful, Aiya." Chiyo embraces me and I feel her berry lips near my neck. I find myself giggling.

"He perks up when I sing to him. It's quite cute," I say.

"A wolf heard your song and it captured his heart. You can sing to the birds and they reply. The forest is your second home. You are special," she says and we head back home.

"I think I might be," I whisper.

***

I use the small knife Hajime gave me to cut off a thin but long lock of hair. Tying it in a secure knot I hide the hair in my obi. I want it to be a surprise. Riku is having his time to himself. I make my way to Hajime's shop. I haven't spoken with him yet.

His brother motions for me to wait while he goes to get Hajime from the back. He looks happy to see me. We both light up and hug each other. His embrace is scented with the embers and metal from his labor filled day.

"Aiya! It's so good to see you. How are you?"

"Happy. I'm really happy, Hajime." My answer pleases him. I think he has wanted me to be happy like this for a long time.

"That's incredible. You look like it," he says. We don't speak for a moment. It's awkward but I let it go. He knows me. I know our history.

"Can I ask you to do something for me?" I break the silence.

"Of course. What is it?" He looks eager.

Hajime takes pride in his work. He is a great swordsmith and friend. That is why he needs to be the one to make this. I pull out the lock of hair and hand it to him. He takes it in his large palm as though it were a small bird.

"Can you make Riku a sword? I want you to make it like how you made mine."

"Yes! I would love to. It will take me a couple weeks. Thank you, Aiya. I am so honored." I put my hand over the lock of hair in his.

"No, thank you. I want to give Riku something really special," I say.

"You give him something special every day." Hajime smiles with his teeth and the corners of his eyes crease up.

"What's that?"

"Your love. It is the most meaningful thing in his life, Aiya." His words make icicles in my lungs.

"You think so?" I don't know why but I feel insecure and it's showing.

"Without a doubt. He loves you so much," says Hajime.

"Sometimes I think I love him more than he loves me."

"I think you both love each other the same amount in different ways."

"How did you get to be so wise?" I raise my eyebrow at him in a joking way but I'm serious.

"From the teachings of my own heart. I listen to it. Over the years it has become my guide. It is where I conjure up my strength," he says.

"You are able to see something most of us can't because you listen to yourself. You trust your heart. I admire that about you. I always have," I say. My admission makes both of us blush.

"The power of your heart is the strongest that I know."

"Thank you, Hajime. You're the best." I wave to him as I exit the shop.

CHAPTER SIXTEEN

When the Moon Rises

Riku and I are in the forest catching snowflakes. I take his hands and he spins me. Twirling around I feel my hair fan out around me. The wind picks it up and blows through the sleeves of my kimono and lifts my inky tresses. I'm wearing the buttercup and cream kimono today. He gives me longing glances but conceals his face. As I spin the snow lands on my eyelashes and I see the world through crystals.

My face aches from smiling. I keep thinking about the day Riku came back for me. It was my sixteenth birthday. I was wearing a yellow sunset kimono. My hair was shorter then. As I plucked the flower petals I would play a game of "Does he love me? Does he not?" and I always landed on "he loves me." Riku has known we'd be together all along. I have faith in him. How could I have ever doubted him? I'm distracted by my happiness and don't notice it at first but then it rings in my ears. The barbaric noise of monkey demons. I must look worried.

"What is it?" Riku's expression changes and he becomes tense. He doesn't like when I look worried or scared.

"Riku, do you hear that?" I ask.

"It's a troop of monkey demons," he says in a gruff tone. I'm afraid but don't want to show it.

"What do we do?" I ask.

"Stay next to me."

The trunks of the trees rumble and the branches shift and crack.

The monkey demons near us and snow falls from the canopy.

"Well, well, well. What do we have here?" says a monkey demon. This one is smaller than the first one I met. The demon monkey king roams my body with his bulbous gray eyes. I see him grab his bulge and eye me with lust.

Refusing to back down I stare up at him with a blank gaze. The monkey king drools as he watches me. He wipes his saliva away with the palm of his hand. Riku is my army. I am not afraid.

"Leave us be!" Riku barks at the monkey king.

Holding onto my hand he keeps me behind him. I watch the troop of monkey demons over his broad shoulders.

"Look, boys. He has something real pretty with him," snarls the monkey king.

Riku lets out a thunderous growl. The cowardly demons hop up into the higher branches and tremble as they should. There's eleven massive monkey demons including the king.

"Don't even think about it," growls Riku. He is baring his canines. His face is still handsome even like this.

"We were searching for some persimmons but I see you have something much sweeter. Get her, boys!" commands the monkey king.

They surround us. Riku pulls me to his side and wraps his muscular arm around me. His sword is drawn. He is prepared to murder them all for me. I stare up at his face, fierce with loyalty. There is nothing he wouldn't do for me.

"She's even prettier up close," grunts one of the monkey men. This one licks his lips and blows me a kiss. Their nostrils flare with want.

"She smells good, too. Like honey," says another.

That's what the other man said. It must be alluring to them. Their tails are long and white. Their hair is the color of snow and they wear it up. Shiny round eyes resembling frozen rivers give me lascivious stares. A taller monkey demon shoves his hand down his trousers and sticks his tongue out at me.

"Back off!"

Riku is growling. He holds me to his side as though I will be ripped away. There is something dark about the way I want to be held like this. He is here and nowhere else. If I am in danger he is right here with me.

"Oh, come on! We'll give her back when we're done," says another.

He makes a salacious gesture at me. Riku's squeezing nearly knocks the wind out of me but I love the way it feels. The burning desire, my soul crushing love, the fire in my heart prepares me for what I'm about to do next. I inhale snow and exhale pink air. There are coals sitting on my pelvic bone and a tingling sensation going up and down my spine.

"You'll have to pry her from my cold, dead hands," says Riku.

He is about to swing his blade but I put up the fire barrier with minimal effort. The heat in my center keeps it burning. He loosens his grip. His jaw has dropped and I see the flames reflecting in his eyes. I have secrets, too.

"How did you do that?" he asks.

"I've been practicing," I say.

The grin won't leave my face. Touching my chest and my face I feel how I am feverish but there is no sweat on my brow. The fire whispers to me. I memorize this new language. It is just for me.

"You did it, Aiya. You protected us," says Riku in awe. He picks me up and kisses me. I could be mistaken but he seems sad.

"I did, didn't I?"

I've never been so proud of myself.

***

The nights are long and we spend our days happily. I've made a new little friend, a flying squirrel. He hides in my hair and I see Riku long to disappear into the ink as well. The squirrel makes friends with Riku and I lose them both. Somehow I'm able to elude my new friend and Riku. I make them both play games with me. It must drive Riku crazy but I'm having fun with him. It's getting late but I make Riku look for me.

We walk home as the sunset tints everything orange and pink. It melts into a rainbow right before it fades into blue and black. Stars shimmer and make me miss Hanako. I hope she's enjoying spending time with her family. Not ready to go inside yet we sit and look towards the heavens. I turn my gaze to the moon. It's the waxing crescent. Does the wolf god control the amount of light we see at night?

"What are you thinking about?" asks Riku. He scoots closer to me.

"I was wondering if the wolf god could see us now." I keep my eyes on the crescent moon.

"I have wondered that for many years," he says.

"Riku, what do you believe in?" I ask.

"I'm not sure. For a long time I thought I didn't believe in anything. The truth is I couldn't believe in a book that told me to kill my father," he says. I wince at his history.

"I thought I was no one but I have been everything. All the changes I've gone through have caused me to question what it means to have faith," I confess.

"What do you mean?" he asks.

"When I was searching for you I began to lose hope. Brother Minoru said to me, 'Have faith, Aiya. Faith is what keeps us alive.' There were days I thought I would die alone in the forest but I repeated what he told me in my head. Over and over. It was what I was thinking when I called your name."

"Were you a nonbeliever?" Riku is inquisitive tonight.

"Yes. After I woke up and saw you I knew someone was watching over me. I have believed ever since," The words sparkle in my lungs and I am grateful to be the one he saved.

"Someone is. The demigod told me so," he says.

This makes me smile and I pull him into the house. The fire is lit and the house is warm. Not that it matters. I am never cold. Riku averts his eyes as I throw off my stormy blue kimono and get into bed.

"Riku?" My breath ruffles the fabric of my pillow.

I wonder if Riku lays in my bed and breathes in the honey scented sheets. Am I irresistible to him?

"What's wrong?" he asks as I wrap my slender arms around him. They cradle him, here in my web of dreams and fate. Stars are my lure. I am the spider.

"Nothing. I just want you close to me," I say.

He embraces me. There are sharp claws along the length of my back. He rests his chin on top of my head. His breathing slows as he drifts off. The rise and fall of his chest is unhurried. My heart beats fast and flutters. It's like a winged beast in my chest.

I hold my breath and try to keep it in. With his arms around me I fall asleep right away. I wake often, though. No nightmares but the gestures of the monkey demon and the voice of the jaguar slither through my mind. I shouldn't bother him when he's sleeping but I do. Nudging his chin so I can kiss his neck I am able to block out the terrible things going on in my head.

"Please, don't." I've been caught.

"Sorry." I kiss him but he doesn't kiss me back. He's too tired.

"It's okay," he whispers.

We sleep for a while but I keep getting intrusive images of Kasai's serpent tongue constricting around me and taste the jaguar's lips on mine. I can't sleep with the musky scent in my mouth. Knowing I shouldn't doesn't prevent me from tasting the roof of Riku's mouth. It's evergreen and snowflakes.

"Stop!" Riku barking at me is jarring and I shrink back. I'm annoying him but all I want is for him to pay attention to me.

"I love you." It's what I say when I am at a loss for words.

"I love you, too." His voice is quiet again.

I try to go back to sleep. The images in my mind startle me and I stare up at the ceiling wondering why they won't go away. I am able to steal sleep in between the thoughts plaguing me. Riku sleeps through everything. I'm jealous of his ability to sleep in peace.

He is sound asleep. I don't want him to be mad at me but I wrap myself around him. My palm rests on his heart and I hold his waist with my leg. His hands are cool but I don't mind. I lay on him and feel protected. Looking at my lover's face I see that he is smiling. I am so curious to know what makes him smile like this. He is here but I am alone. Careful not to be too loud I sing in a whisper.

> *The wolf was once lonely*
> *But never again*
> *He is my one*
> *He is my only*

I thought he was asleep but Riku's lips are on mine. He kisses me so intensely I keep my eyes open at first. We are fire and ice. I unbutton his shirt and taste his tongue on mine. His hands are all over me and in my hair. His touch ignites a blaze. It frightens me but I like it. A willing participant in hunter and prey. He's inside me and for once I don't think Riku is somewhere else.

*****

The birdsongs wake me but I don't open my eyes. I reach for him. He's here. Resting my hand on his shoulder I fall back asleep. This time I feel peaceful. My slumber is fulfilling and long. I don't want to wake up. I want to stay like this forever. There is the lingering suspicion of being watched. I open my eyes and find Riku looking at me. I smile which always makes him smile. I kiss him a thousand times until he asks me to stop.

"I can't breathe," he says. It makes me want to kiss him more but I don't.

"Sorry."

"Don't say that," Riku is being stern with me again. He touches my face and makes sure I'm listening.

"What?" I'm confused.

"That you're sorry," he says.

"Why?" I ask.

"Because you never have to say you're sorry to me. Okay?"

"Okay."

I kiss the tip of his nose and lay back down. Riku is a mystery to me. A dark sky, an eternal ocean, secretive and deep. Even though I've been sleeping for hours I drift off. No more lewd voices in my head. I no longer see the jaguar's emerald eyes or taste his musky animalistic tongue. This must be what it's like to be free.

When I reach for Riku I expect him to be gone but he's still here. He pulls me towards him. I can't help myself and nudge his chin to kiss his neck. He doesn't stop my advance and he is mine again. We sleep tangled up in each other until midday.

"I'll be right back," he says and gets up.

"Where are you going?" I ask.

"It's going to be a surprise." Riku gives me a sly but genuine smile.

"I like surprises."

I sleep on his side of the bed and pretend to be in his cloak until he comes back. He is with me in a different way. I wait for him but not like before. When he gets home he is already smiling. I wonder what it is making him smile like that.

We talk about nothing and everything. The sun is about to set. I haven't got dressed but I wrap myself in the blanket and run outside giggling. Riku observes me with a mischievous smirk. I've never seen him look at me like this. The powdery snow melts as I walk. Riku comes up beside me and picks me up. Watching the sunset together I feel different. I am whole. Riku's smile is beautiful but striking. I need to know why.

"What are you thinking about?" I ask him. He smiles like he has a secret.

"You."

"What about me?" I try to get out of his grasp but he won't put me down. He dips me and we rub noses.

"How much I love you," he says.

"How much do you love me?"

"More than anything."

"Really?" I ask.

"Yes, really." He puts me down and we admire the sparkling snow. The moon rises. The hair on the back of my neck rises with it. I rest my hand there and half smile.

"Riku, can I ask you something?"

"You can ask me anything," he says in his gruff but quiet voice. I wait a moment and take a deep breath.

"Where do you go?" I ask, avoiding eye contact.

"What do you mean?" Riku kneels down to see me better. He is taller than everyone in the village. I am lost in his shadow most of the time.

"There are times we are together but I know you are far away. Where do you go when you hide from me?" The words are crisp.

He ponders my question for quite some time. Does he not want to tell me? Perhaps he doesn't know.

"I disappear inside myself. I'll try harder not to. I'm sorry." He puts his arms around my waist.

"Is it because of me?" I ask.

"No. It's because of me," he says. Riku looks up at me even though it pains him to do so.

"You don't have to hide from me. I love you just the way you are."

My words appear to break something in Riku and he grabs me again.

"Why?" he asks.

"Why what?"

The moon is further away tonight but I think I hear it calling to me. I keep my eyes on it. What is the wolf god doing right now?

"Why do you love me?" His question is easy to answer but hard to explain. I'm not sure what to say.

"There's a hundred different reasons why I love you," I say. Riku takes my hand and holds it like a bird that will fly away.

"How is it that I am the one you love?" he asks.

"Because you're special."

CHAPTER SEVENTEEN

In the Depths of Night

"Are you ready?" Riku asks me.

I nod my head. Today is cold but sunny. The sky is bright blue. There are no clouds or wind. He ties his obi around my eyes as a blindfold. I feel him race through the forest faster than ever. There is the ripping sound of bark coming off the trees from his cloak hitting the trunk at the right angle.

"Riku, where are we going?"

"I told you, it's a surprise," he says. I can't see it but I know he's smiling.

"I like surprises." I whisper.

"Do you trust me?" he asks.

"Yes."

I feel him jump. We hit the ground with a loud crack. Mud and snow fly around us, I can smell it and hear it when it lands. We go a bit further. He slows to a walk. The sun is on my face and I hear cranes passing over us. Setting me down with gentle hands I feel excited.

"Keep your eyes closed," he says. I feel him removing the obi but don't open my eyes.

"Can I open them now?" I ask.

Riku doesn't answer my question. I know he is standing next to me. Where are we? Right when I think he isn't going to say anything he takes me by the shoulders and turns me around.

"Okay, you can open them now," he says.

I open my eyes to a field of peonies. The snowy hills are lined with blue and white roses. The flowers go on forever. I can't see beyond the swooping hills of pink and purple. It's the most gorgeous place I've ever seen. It can't be compared to anywhere else.

"Riku, how did you find this place?" I gasp.

"I wanted to find somewhere special for you."

I feel the effervescence flow through my veins and I take off running. In my excitement I grab a blue rose and it pricks me. A single blood drop runs down my palm. I don't care though. I'm too enthralled.

Riku is chasing me. I know I can outrun him so I slow down. It makes me happy to see him come after me. There is a morbid lust for it within my heart. I want him to look for me when I hide. How I wish for him to hunt me down and find me. He grabs me and swings me around. We kiss and I give him the rose that has a red stain on the thorn.

"It's beautiful here," I sigh and breathe in the decadent floral scent.

"Nothing and no one is as beautiful as you though." Riku doesn't talk a lot but it's poetic anytime he does.

"Really?"

"Yes, really."

He takes my hand and we begin strolling through the pink hills. The petals are silky frost. I braid my hair and decorate it with the blossoms. My hair is long enough to hold more than a dozen peonies. I'm wearing the yellow kimono Riku loves. I didn't paint my lips today but I feel pretty.

"I've been wanting to ask you something." Riku's deep voice behind me stops me in my tracks. I turn around, still twirling my hair.

"What is it?" I'm shocked to see Riku get on one knee and pull out a gold ring.

"Aiya, will you marry me?" His question is all I've wanted to hear for three years.

I stare at him and the ring. This doesn't feel real. Is this a dream? Riku is distant from me but we are never far apart. Tears spill down my face but not because I'm sad. I'm happy to know all my doubts will be erased. I am the one he loves.

He is eye level with me on his knees and I put my arms around him. My tears touch his cheek and fall onto his shoulder. His arms were slack but they are now tight around my waist. When he holds me it feels like he will never let me go. Smiling from ear to ear I whisper to him.

"I've been waiting for you to ask me," I laugh through my tears.

"How long have you been waiting?" he asks.

"Since my sixteenth birthday," I say. Riku pulls back to study my face. He has tears in his eyes, too. His surprised look is my favorite.

"Would you have said yes to me then? I would have been a stranger to you."

"I didn't think of you as a stranger. I saw you every night in my dreams," I say but Riku cuts me off and kisses me.

With a small pounce I knock Riku into the snow. We lay in the white abyss and admire the gold ring on my finger. It's my anchor. I will cherish him forever.

The days where I'm a ghost he brings me back to life. As he disappears inside himself I will be the one to find him. He is my winter, the evergreen forest where I reside. On sunny days he is a god. In the fall he is a thief, stealing color from the leaves.

Riku mangages to be everything but thinks he is no one. He has powerful magic and can sit next to me but be a thousand miles away. My song calls him back. He is my captive audience.

I've watched the way he sacrifices pieces of himself for everybody else. Riku is everyone's hero. There is nothing he wouldn't do to help. His demeanor is dauntless. He seems unbreakable but is quite shy and easily startled. Everything about him surprises me. On rainy days he is my shelter. We are a perfect storm.

"I know what I would wish for," he announces.

"What?" I ask.

"For this moment to last forever."

I look at Riku. His blissful face, the ring on my finger, the field of flowers around us is perfect. I want this moment to last forever, too. For him I will smile everyday. I will tell him I love him over and over until he believes me. I don't know if it's possible but I want to love Riku so intensely he loves himself.

***

Riku doesn't leave my side very much anymore. As soon as he does I dart out the door and rush into the forest. The house can't contain me. The village can't either. I am lightning as I tear up the snowy floor of the woods. I'm laughing and spinning. Everything is too good to be true. The past four mornings I wake up and look at my hand to make sure it's real. I took it off to inspect it. Inside is the engraving *"Nothing without you."* I asked Riku what it meant. He said it's his people's demonic canon. That no one could exist without the other but he says it's meant for just me.

In the core of my soul I feel a fire burning inside. I'm intoxicated by the reality of Riku's love. He proves it to me daily but when he proposed I knew he really loved me. He is not the type to do something without meaning. The gold buttons of his shirt and bodysuit are missing. He must have used them to make it. Riku's ability to be sweet without expecting praise is precious. I've stopped at the hot spring. I don't want to get it but I want to be near it. The water is clear and steamy. I look at my reflection and examine my small face splashed with freckles. Long lashes tickle my cheeks and brow bone. Riku said nothing and no one was as beautiful as me.

"Hey Special. What's got you looking so happy?" It's Bara.

She leans against the boulder to my left. Her arms are crossed but her face is relaxed. I hold out my left hand and show her the ring. Narrow green eyes widen and her red mouth opens.

"Wow! Congratulations!" Bara takes my hand and studies it, "I'm glad to know he isn't alone. You won't be alone anymore either."

"What do you mean?"

"I see you in here by yourself while your friends and fiance wait for you in the village. You are like me. We want to roam free. Be different. It's okay to take space but don't forget to show your affection to others," she says. The red coyote woman speaks with authority.

"I always thought it was Riku who ran away but it's been me all along."

My realization is slate clouds on a perfect day. Bara unfolds her arm and places her hands on my elbows.

"I didn't mean to upset you. I am only an observer. What do I know?"

"Your insight is helpful. I should take better care of the ones I love," I say.

"And take better care of yourself." Bara lifts her well defined eyebrow at me.

"What?" I don't know what she is talking about.

"I've seen the monkey demons and the jaguars follow you. They are hungry for a taste of honey. Be careful out here. Wolf boy won't always be around to save you," she says.

"I can take care of myself."

"I know you can. Just be wary, okay?"

The red coyote lets me go and scampers into the ferns and cedars. I think about what Bara said as I jump into a tree. Sitting on a high branch I watch hares and shrews scurry past. A snowy owl swoops down and lifts up a mouse in one smooth motion. The breeze is harsh and cold but I am enjoying my spot in the trees. There are numerous birds singing all at once. I am about to call out to them but they go quiet.

There are no more rodents darting across the ground. Every bird resists flapping their wings. I can't see a single creature. The deer do not move. Frail brown legs with hooves appear restrained. I stand up and press my back into the trunk of the tree. What is lurking in here?

Jumping into a darker part of the tree I crouch. I hide in my place in the pines and wait to see the intruder. A crane sings in the distance but there is no reply. Snow doesn't fall and there is not even the flutter of an insect. It's an enormous quiet filling this part of the forest. I feel it before I see it. Below me the branches tremble ever so slightly. I make sure I am hidden and peek out to see who it is. It's a jaguar.

This one has sky blue eyes. His hair is shaggy and dark brown. The tail moves back and forth making swishing noises. He wears red trousers. His chest is broad and hairy. The shoulders have black spots and markings on the tops of them. I see he is looking for something. His head turns back and forth on his muscular neck. The ears twitch and listen for any clue as to where I am.

"Dammit! I know she is somewhere around here," he grumbles.

The tiny chirps and purring in his throat sickens me. Thankfully he doesn't look up to where I am. He continues flying through the lower branches. Making sure he is gone I step out from the shadows. That was close. It's getting late. Riku will be waiting for me.

Traveling through the canopy I make my way home to the one I love. He seeks me out now. Things are different. Riku doesn't tell me what to do but he likes me in yellow so I wear those kimonos a lot. He asks me to sing to him. I've been making up new songs every day.

The wolf and I
Are fire and ice
My love for him
Will never die

Riku greets me as I'm singing up the path to my house. Picking me up he spins me around. I hold onto his shoulders and take in his gorgeous smile that lights me up.

"Did you hear my song for you?"

"Yes. I wait for them," he says.

***

Singing Riku awake has become part of my daily routine. It makes him so happy to hear my voice. He says he waits for me to sing as the birds do. When he wakes he is mine. Daylight slips away without a trace during this time in winter. It's getting dark already but we have spent the day in bed. There is nowhere else I'd rather be.

"I wish I approached you that day." He's twirling the ring on my finger. I grip his hand with mine.

"I like things just the way they are," I assure him.

"You do?" he asks.

"Yes." I close my eyes. "What would you have said to me if you did approach me?" I ask. He's still playing with the ring.

"Hi," he says. All of a sudden I start laughing. I don't think I've ever laughed this hard. I look at Riku who appears to be hurt and confused. I wish to explain myself but I can't. Riku watches me with amusement and joins in my laughter. Covering my mouth I try to stifle my giggle.

"Sorry," I say and wipe the grin from my face.

"What would you have said to me?" he asks. I stare up at the ceiling and think about it for a minute.

"There you are. I've been waiting for you–" as I say the words he kisses me and is mine once again.

***

I haven't told anyone but there's something stirring inside me. Low in my belly below my navel. My fingers graze the stars and there is a pulse so subtle I almost ignore it. But I can't. For the past ten days I have felt it growing stronger. I should tell Riku but for some reason I've wanted to keep it to myself. I love them and I want to know them first.

I plan on telling Riku soon. I want the moment to be perfect. I dream of seeing how happy it makes him. No moment has felt right but I will find it. Holding myself and swaying with glee I hear a familiar voice behind me.

"Hey Special." It's the red coyote.

"Hi Bara." She looks at me with her sly eyes and gives me a wide grin.

"What you got there?" She signals towards my hands resting on my stomach.

"A secret," I say with a smirk. Bara and I communicate with our eyes and she lets out a laugh fit for the gods.

"The wolf demon has it all. Who would have thought?" She puts her hands on her hips and studies me.

"I haven't told him yet." Bara's expression changes.

"Why not?" she asks. Her tone is sad. I haven't heard her speak this way.

"I don't know. I guess I wanted to love them first. I'm going to tell him tonight." I wasn't going to but the way the red coyote is looking at me makes me feel I must say such.

"I'm happy for you. For all of you. Now get out of here and go back to your man," says Bara and she waves me out with her freckled arms. I smile at her comment and make my way to leave. Now I have to tell him.

I get home as the sun is rising. He's still asleep. I crawl back into bed and pretend I didn't get up. When he wakes we go to my favorite place in the forest and find my squirrel friend. I named him Niko. He plays in my hair and I dance around the cedars. The wolf demon sees my companion nuzzle my neck and look jealous. I take my little friend and hand him to Riku who holds the small creature with care.

Playing in the snow I think about how I'm going to tell him. Spinning fans my hair. I am ink and stars. Riku is pine and ice. What will the child inside me be? I hold out my hands and Riku gives Niko back to me. I kiss the top of his fuzzy head and he flies from my palm into the trees. It makes me laugh which makes Riku laugh. He tells me he loves me and picks me up to carry me home.

I'm making tea as Riku is falling asleep. I should have told him earlier. Maybe he'll wake up. He's exhausted after chasing me around and making sure I don't get hurt. I try to be on my best behavior but I'm having fun. Riku's face is relaxed. His normally tense shoulders are slack as well. I get into bed and fall asleep even though I can't stop touching the quiver beneath the stars. I hope Riku doesn't notice. Taking his hand to my heart I close my eyes and enter bliss.

I wake up to being touched. Riku is lifting my hair and kissing me. The fire is low but bright enough to illuminate the room. Yellow shadows dance against the wooden walls. It is here and now in the dim light that I want to tell Riku a secret.

"Are you awake?" I ask.

"Yes." I turn around and kiss his nose. This makes the corners of his mouth curve up.

"Riku, do you like surprises?" I ask.

Riku doesn't meet my gaze as he ponders my question. I see him take it very seriously. That's one of the many things I love about him. He is not one to be thoughtless.

"Yes," he says.

His answer is sincere. Untying my kimono I pull it open and take his hand that's twice the size of mine to place it over my navel. To my dismay Riku doesn't smile like I thought he would. Instead he recoils and I feel a thousand stinging insects in my chest.

"I'm sorry. I thought you would be happy."

I sit up. Now I'm really upset. I thought this would be the best moment of his life. The pulse beats softly in the depths of night. A gift from the gods. It seemed like everything he would want. Riku reaches for me and touches the stars below my navel. This time his hand lingers there.

"I am happy. I just wasn't expecting this so soon is all. Come here," he says as he pulls me down next to him. Maybe I am just upset but I can't tell if he is being genuine. His hand doesn't leave where it rests on my flat stomach. It makes me feel better as do his words, "Don't say sorry. Especially about this."

Not knowing what to do I put my hand on his. The ring is an anchor. Gold weighs heavy on my heart. I want to feel our baby together but I also want to cry. For some reason I wish I kept it to myself. Then I realize the moment wasn't perfect or happy the way I envisioned it in my head.

CHAPTER EIGHTEEN

Red

I've been waiting to tell Chiyo. Even though she will be most excited I feel strange announcing my happiness to her. She is in love as she has wanted to be since I've known her. I thought she would be married with a child first. It seems wrong. I know she won't be mad but I bide my time.

I can't wait to tell Hanako. How her face will brighten when she hears the news. I imagine her ears will bounce with glee and her nose will wrinkle with her smile. I told Brother Minoru first. He has been like a father to me. The one who held me after Riku set me down. The face I saw as I opened my eyes. I remember his soft voice calling to me. "Please, open your eyes." Like magic I did. There were shiny brown eyes looking back at me. They smiled and he said "There you are." Brother Minoru cried as I had expected.

Lady Kiyori didn't give much of a reaction but gave Riku a knowing glance. They speak without words and I can't decipher their hidden meanings. Natsume, Hiromi, and Daina shrieked and rubbed my belly with enthusiasm. They smiled with their teeth and their eyes creased in the corners. I don't know how I ever thought they weren't my friends.

We're heading to Hajime's shop. I'm nervous to tell him. I decide to tell Chiyo and him at the same time. That way it's all out there. Riku is nervous, more nervous than I. He holds me close to his side. It's like he worries a slight breeze or butterfly will take me away. I don't protest. He is protective as he should be. As we near the swordsmith's, my heart echoes in my ears. There is a rush of blood to my face and it feels hot and flushed.

"Riku! Aiya!" Chiyo is standing outside the shop. Her dark hair and berry lips are bright against the fresh fallen snow. Stormy eyes sparkle and my knees are weak.

"Hi Chiyo," Riku greets her first. I think he feels more comfortable around Chiyo than the others. My best friend takes a handful of hair and twirls it like when we were kids.

"What did you want to tell me?" she asks.

Chiyo looks at me with those morning glories and I want to burst. Over her shoulder I see Hajime step out of the shop. His hairline is soaked but the smile he wears is wholesome and sugary.

"Aiya, Riku! How are you?" asks Hajime.

"Never been better," I reply. I feel Riku tighten his snug grip around me.

"You said you had something to tell us," says Hajime who eyes Riku and then me.

Violet petals see right through me. I wonder if anyone else notices. Chiyo and Hajime watch me as though I am the world. They are my family.

"I'm pregnant," I sigh.

His jaw drops. My best friend and Hajime look down at my lower belly guarded by my left hand. At first there are no words but they smile. Then it happens. Chiyo jumps and claps. She is a joyful person. The voice she speaks in is bells and breezy days. Stormy eyes sparkle and rain pours out little by little.

"That's great news! Congratulations! You two must be so happy," says my sweet best friend. She is pure. Untouched by the darkness of jealousy or rage. Chiyo wants this for me.

"It brings me happiness to see you two start your family," says Hajime. He looks at Riku and then back at me. The color purple is deeper than the sky and the sea. It takes me somewhere else.

"Riku, what do you want to name your baby?" asks Chiyo.

"I want Aiya to pick their name." Riku hasn't spoken much since I've told him I'm pregnant. It eases me when he does. I embrace him to say I like that answer. He loosens his steel grip on me.

"I'm not sure yet. It will come to me." I think about Takara. His name seemed obvious. My mother let me choose it. Father said it was a perfect name.

"Riku, do you want a boy or a girl?" asks Hajime. I want a boy but don't say anything. Curiosity makes me listen intently for Riku's reply.

"I just want them to be healthy and happy," he says. I stand on the tips of my toes to kiss him. This makes him relax and he gives me more slack.

"You will all be happy," says Hajime.

He puts out his hand to feel my stomach. I take it without hesitation and place it where the pulse is. It's quiet at first and I can't place the sound but Riku has a growl in his throat. The kind a dog has right before it's about to bite.

I know he has certain habits but I'm shocked he would be this untrusting of my friends. Hajime would never do anything to hurt me or our baby. The three of us lock eyes and we decide to let it go. Riku is allowed his feelings.

"Sorry," he mumbles.

Chiyo reaches out and touches me as well. Riku is holding me too tight again. The subtle surge of life inside me moves and I see Chiyo and Hajime widen their eyes.

"Wow," says Hajime."

"What?" Riku barks out the word. He wants to leave because he is uncomfortable but I want to share this moment with them.

"It's just so beautiful," says Hajime.

Chiyo takes a step back to hold his shoulders. Petals and rain clouds hover over the stars. I get a twinge in my chest. Chiyo is in love with Hajime. It pleases me to see the two of them like this yet I must try to resist my subtle irritation. Things would have never worked out between me and Hajime but I feel betrayed.

"We better get going. I'll see you two tomorrow. Goodbye!" I say and wave to my friends, but feel annoyed.

Twirling the ring on my finger and placing my palm to the steady tap of my baby interrupts the intrusive thoughts but I'm ashamed.

My other hand reaches for Riku and we walk home together in silence. I'm worried he saw my reaction. Perhaps he is mad at me.

Once we're inside I light the fire. Using my comb I brush the black ink smooth and straight. I wash my face and put on my powder that smells like lilies. Riku seems less tense but isn't very talkative. He says he's happy but deep down, deeper than the pink silk where the pulse is, I sense Riku wishes he was somewhere else without me. Without us.

"Riku, are you going to come to bed?" I ask.

"In a little bit. I have a lot on my mind," he says. I do as well. The emotionally harrowing experiences the last few weeks have left me too tired to argue, or beg for him to lay next to me.

"Okay."

I turn to my side and press my fingers into the shooting stars. It lasts only a second but it startles me. I think about running away in the night, just the two of us.

***

"There you are, Katan."

"My name is Aiya. Get off of me!" Kasai is pulling me by my wrist. I try to hit him with my other hand but his body is made of stone. He looks different. The fur of the bear is gone and he now covers his face with the skull of a vulture. His chest is bare and smooth. I chide myself for staring. What's wrong with me?

"Come here, my love. Why do you fight me?"

"I'm not yours. Let me go!"

I try to rip myself from his grasp but I can't. His massive hands are strong and made of steel. Huge muscles shift under his tan skin. The veins in his arm protrude.

"I'm better than the wolf boy in every way. Why did you choose him?"

Kasai's voice is thunderous and menacing. He continues to bring me deeper into The Underworld. His long red cloak drags on the ground. It has tears at the hem but he doesn't pick it up. Black boots kick up crimson dust.

"I will always choose him!"

Attempting to escape his hold on me I thrash. I only get a few steps away before I fall. Laying on the ground I feel the blanket of his black shadow. It's ice cold. He pounces on me and grabs my neck with a menacing fist.

"Not for long," he hisses as the serpent tongue enters my mouth.

I wake up and cough. My hair is drenched in sweat. It's sticking to my face, back, and chest. Riku is sleeping next to me. I look around to take in my surroundings. My teapot, the scented powder, and my clothes comfort me. That is until I notice the sickly ache in the pink silk.

With a shaky hand I pull back the white sheets. Blood. So much blood. I gasp and to my despair I feel more scarlet fluid gush out. The fair skin of my thighs is slathered in glossy red liquid. My white blanket and mat are soaked as well. I reach for Riku but notice the blood all over my hands and stop myself.

I try to say his name but I can't. Instead I cry hot salty tears and let the misery consume me. Is Kasai really back? Or was it just a nightmare? I defeated him. He shouldn't be able to hurt me anymore. Is it possible for him to invade my dreams from beyond? I can't stop the rain and it stings my face as it storms. A shiver runs up my spine. It causes another spasm and I almost cry out. Ruby streams cascade down my legs and I know I have to wake him up.

"Riku?" He sits up with his eyes closed.

"What's wrong?" as he asks the question I see his nose wrinkle up and his face crumple.

Opening his eyes he examines my face and then looks down. My hands and thighs are covered in blood. I try to wipe it away but there's so much of it. There's sheer scarlet on my knuckles and under my fingernails. Every time I look in between my legs there's more blood. The scent is coppery and shiny. It pricks the air with its metal.

"Riku, I'm really scared."

Looking at my left hand I see there is blood on my ring, too. Everything is red.

"It's okay. I'm here," says Riku in his quiet but caring way.

He wraps me in the blanket and picks me up. He pauses to inspect the mat. Underneath is sopping wet with crimson liquid. I wince seeing life leave me in the form of red rivers on my legs.

"What should we do?" I sob.

Why is this happening to me? I thought I was special. Do the gods not want me and Riku to have a baby? For some reason I think about Takara which makes me cry even more.

"I'm going to get you some help."

Riku manages to be strong when we are falling apart. How is it that he is so brave? I can't bear the pain. I've had too much taken from me. I still have a family but my parents and siblings are dead. Now I'm sure my baby is dead and I don't think I can stand to lose something as precious as a child. Riku walks on even ground as a spirit. We arrive at Lady Kiyori's.

"What's wrong?" she asks.

Riku and Lady Kiyori speak without sound and he steps in. He sets me down but still holds me. I don't think he will let go even if Lady Kiyori asks him to. There are many things that need to be said but I can't say a thing. I do most of the talking for us. Right now I am speechless.

The woman who raised me like her own daughter begins to wash away the blood that is all over me. She wipes away the red rivers and blots at the stains on my knees and thighs. The warm water and soft touch soothe me but I'm still sad. My baby couldn't have survived this. There is too much of me missing.

"Aiya woke up like this," says Riku. Lady Kiyori feels my forehead and flushed cheeks. Her face is worried. Not a good sign.

"Has she shown any indication of sickness? Complaints of any pain?" she asks. Riku looks at me with loving eyes and I shake my head "no."

"Last night she felt warmer than usual," he says.

"Aiya, have you been feeling distressed or overwhelmed?" My voice is lost to me at first but I shake my head "no."

"No. I've been really happy," I say.

The waterfalls can't be contained and it flows from my eyes to my chin and lands at the stars of my collar bone. My crying is violent and more blood is pushed from the pink silk. Out of the corner of my eye I see Riku is also crying.

His hold on me is powerful. I do not wish to escape but I know I never could if I wanted to. Gentle hands dab at the new blood that is bright red. She refills the bowl with more hot water and removes the last of the scarlet ink.

"Riku, are you okay?" asks Lady Kiyori.

"I'm okay," he says.

Riku is hiding in my hair. It's nice but I feel him crying into the blackest night. I'm sure Lady Kiyori feels sorry for us both. She is a kind and caring person. There is no reason for him to be ashamed but I know he is. I smell something herbal and citrusy. Lady Kiyori hands me a cup of tea.

"Here, it will make you feel better."

I take the steamy beverage and sip. It's good but tart. The back of my head is wet with Riku's tears. I wonder how long he will hide from me? If I am the one he loves, why does he put distance between us? There is a space from me to him and in that span I grow to love him more but long to have him here with me.

I've never been in love. It is magical but confusing. I wake up in the night and my head has doubts pouring out of the top. Then there are days like the day he proposed and I know he is meant to be my forever. Riku pulls me closer and I fall asleep to the sound of Lady Kiyori tossing the red ink into the snow.

CHAPTER NINETEEN

He Reminds Me of You

There's a hand on my stomach but it's not Riku's. It's much larger and tan.

"Don't touch me!" I scream. As I aim to fight him I am yanked back. There are chains around my wrists.

"What? I can't touch my own child?"

Kasai removes the vulture skull. Thick black hair falls over his shoulders. It's almost as long as mine. He's kneeling down and smirking at me. I want to rip the hand that's caressing me off with my fangs.

"It's Riku's! I'd never have your child," I hiss.

Bile comes up to the back of my throat. The idea of him inside me makes me want to die.

"But I'm already inside you, Katan. You'll see," he says with that wicked smile.

His face is young and handsome. I find myself wanting to put my palm to his cheekbone. It disgusts me.

I wake to Riku shaking me.

"Is something wrong?" I ask. The last time I saw Kasai we almost lost our baby. Lady Kiyori said they were okay but I'm paranoid and protective.

"No, but you need to eat. Here, Lady Kiyori wants you to drink this."

He hands me a cup of the citrusy tea and a skewered fish. I lean on him and eat a little. It's good but I feel sick. I appreciate Riku's efforts to make sure me and the baby are okay.

"Thank you," I rasp.

I haven't told him what keeps me up at night. Why I am so restless but tired.

"You don't have to thank me. I should have been doing this before," he says.

"I like when you take care of me." I am happy but feel cursed. Is my father selling my soul again down in The Underworld? Even if he did, I know Riku would go down there to get me. I have faith in him.

"I like it, too."

***

Riku told me I shouldn't be dancing in the snow or jumping in the cedars. I agree. I want our baby more than anything. There is nothing I wouldn't give up for them. I tell Riku I'm going to hang out with friends which is partly true. I hang out long enough to seem like I was there but I'm distracted. Chiyo's love for Hajime is great, they are perfect for each other. Yet I have the sensation of glowing green envy beneath the skin sitting next to her and listening to her cheerful chatter.

I invite Riku but he declines. He says he has more surprises for me. I like surprises and let him be. After I have tea and talk with Haru and Chiyo I say I have to meet Riku which is the lie. I go into the forest to find solace by myself the way he does. I don't run, I walk this time. Guarding my pregnancy with my left hand I wander into the shadowy parts of the oak trees.

How can I tell Riku what I dream about? It horrifies me. I have a feeling it's going to get worse. I don't want to lose our baby. Did the dream cause me to bleed or was it mere coincidence? I'm not sure what to think. What do I do?

"Hey," it's the husky female voice of the red coyote. She's leaning against one of the oaks. A stream of light comes through the thick branches and highlights her jade green eyes.

"Hi," I whisper. I'm not up for talking.

"What's wrong, Special?" She approaches me and puts her hands on her hips, "I thought I told you to go be with your man."

Bara winks at me in a playful manner that would delight me on any other day but right now I am glum.

"I don't think he's very excited about the baby," I admit.

Saying the words aloud hurts and I reach for the stars to protect them.

"Hey! Why would you say that? I'm sure he's happy. Men are weird about pregnancy," says Bara in a sisterly tone.

"He's protective and takes care of me. We both cried when we thought we lost our baby but I have a feeling he would rather be somewhere else by himself."

The sentence is tinged with venom. Bara notices. She softens her stance and steps closer to me. Taking my face in her beautiful hands she examines me. Staring into my eyes, gazing at the stars, she stares at my mouth so long I think she is going to kiss me.

"You are a sad girl but don't need to be. You hold the world captive but do not know it. A girl loved by many. I see it now," her low voice is cryptic and strange.

"What do you see?" I ask.

"Love is the most powerful force in the world. But it tempts the darkness. Don't give into the darkness, Aiya." She lets me go and scampers off. The tall grass sways from her swift movement.

It's dark and I am sure Riku is going to scold me. To my surprise he is already asleep. Even if I am mad at him I can't be upset when he's sleeping. He looks too sweet. I get into bed and kiss his nose. He doesn't wake up but it makes me happy anyway. As soon as my arms wrap around him everything goes black.

"There's my wife." Kasai's tongue is slithering over his teeth.

"I am not your wife!"

"Are you sure?"

He removes the vulture skull. His eyes are my eyes staring back at me. Our connection is strong but I resent it. I look down to see I am in a white kimono. It's short in the front, exposing my thighs, and long in the back. It drags on for eternity.

Snowy silk is tinted rose and ruby from The Underworld's dust. Kasai's eyes are all over me. I'm holding a bouquet of black roses and my hand is bleeding.

"No. This isn't real. I defeated you!"

I throw down the flowers and rip off the gold ring. It bounces at his feet and he picks it up. He towers over me with his vulture skull and freezing shadow.

"You belong to me. So does the baby in your womb," he hisses at me and puts the ring back on. I don't fight him.

"It's not yours." I can't help but start crying. Kasai puts a huge tan hand to my temple and another to my navel.

"Let me show you," his deep voice lulls me into a daze and I see it.

The pulse in the pink silk. It's small beating makes me smile but it fades as soon as I see their face. It's Kasai's face. I open my eyes.

"No!" I scream and begin hitting Kasai even though it doesn't do anything to him.

"Yes, Katan. Your body, your mind, your soul, it's all mine."

I wake up to Riku shaking me.

"What is it, Riku?" I'm worried I said Kasai's name in my sleep.

"You're burning up. Do you feel okay?"

"I've been having bad dreams," I admit.

"About what?" he asks.

"About him." I can't bear to tell him the truth.

"What happens in them?" he asks.

"I don't want to talk about it," I never say no. I always let him win. But I can't bring myself to say what I saw.

"Aiya, please. Tell me." Now Riku is raising his voice and scaring me.

"No," I say. The word is harsh like a teapot that breaks into a hundred pieces.

"Please, I'm begging you. I'm right here, Aiya. Please, tell me."

He's not going to stop. Riku is the love of my life, without him I would die. I can't lie.

"I dream about Kasai being my baby's father. It disgusts me, Riku. I wake up in the middle of the night and want to die thinking about it."

If it were acceptable I would cut myself just to bleed out the fire demon's blood flowing through me.

"But you know it's not true. He's gone, you defeated him. It's just us now," he says. Riku is sincere. He wants to be here for me. It must be hard being courageous all the time.

"I know. They scare me though. They scare me more than anything," I whisper.

Riku gets out of bed and takes a vial out of his cloak. He puts a couple drops into a cup of water for me.

"I was told this helps with fevers," he says. I take the cup. I can't help but smile. Riku tilts his head the way a puppy does when it's confused. "What?" he asks.

"Nothing." I don't want to make him feel bad.

"Please, tell me." The sad eyes get me every time.

"I just like seeing you like this," I say. Maybe Riku does want us. I've been worried he doesn't care but he does. He shows it in the quiet way most people would never know how to see.

"Like what?" he asks. His head tilts again. I smile to myself and hide it with the teacup.

"Fatherly. You seem happy."

"I am happy," he says.

His words are liquid gold. He lays down in my lap and puts his ear to the stars and listens for the heartbeat. I sip on my tea and watch him fall asleep. Riku smiles and seems to perk up hearing the melody of life play for him as though he's the only one. Could this be his new favorite song?

***

"I love you," the words are wicked and wrong coming from Kasai.

"I won't say it."

"Yes you will," with that he shoves his tongue in my mouth. It wriggles and leaves a bitter taste on my lips. I want to vomit.

"I love you," the words come out clean and crisp.

What? Why did I just say that? Kasai's smirk is a full blown grin. He's smiling with his teeth that are sharp and plentiful.

"That's my girl."

"I'm not your girl," I snarl.

"You've been my girl for a long time, Katan."

I wake up and want to die. Riku is still sleeping. Everything he does annoys me. The past three days have been unbearable. I feel hot and feverish. Riku touches my forehead and says I feel okay. I think he is lying and being neglectful. To get out of my bad mood I put on the new kimono he had made for me. It's buttercup yellow and scarlet. I loved it a few days ago but right now it irritates me. Riku's sleeping face makes me feel guilty. I chide myself on my behavior.

We go for a walk after he wakes. I need to clear my head. Lately I've been shouting at Riku and he seems frightened of me. We never fight. If we do, it lasts for a short amount of time. There hasn't been much to fight about, but now I want to fight about everything. The heat is boiling hot under the stars. My face and collar bone are tinted with magnolias. I get the crazy idea to run. Maybe that would make me feel better. Grinning to myself I go to take off but Riku grabs me.

"Let me go!" I scream. My voice is hoarse from screaming at Riku.

"You said you wouldn't do this anymore, Aiya!"

He is cross now. Riku has let me shout at him for three days but it's wearing on his nerves.

"I want to have fun. You never let me have fun anymore!" I'm being difficult and pulling away. I thrash but my lover is far stronger than I.

"Please, stop. I don't want you to hurt yourself," he says. His tone is soft but his grip is iron clad. It's hurting me and I trash more to dig in deeper.

"Let me go!" His steel hold on me tightens.

"Why are you doing this to me?" he asks.

Riku kneels down to see me better. His sad puppy dog eyes stare into mine that are full of fire and rage.

"I was going to ask you the same question," I hiss. For some reason I can't contain my anger.

"What?" Riku looks at me shocked.

"First you don't come back. Then you get to control everything I do! What gives you the right?" I yell.

The words I've been dying to say but never could fall out piece by piece and cut him up with their glass.

"Aiya, I'm sorry. I–"

"You're always sorry!" I shout again and it startles him.

He lets me go and I take off faster than I ever have. Fast enough so Riku and Kasai can't get me.

"Aiya! Come back here!"

He keeps calling my name but I fly through the cedars and reach for the stars.

***

"There she is, boys!" It's the monkey king again.

"Get away from me!" I snarl. I throw fire from my palms and it hits the ground by their feet.

"Take her down!" screams one of the monkey men.

"I won't let you," I say and put up the fire barrier.

Their grunting and shrill noises cease and I put the wall down. They're gone but the voices and intrusive images remain. I continue to run through the snow hoping to rid myself of the repulsive things in my head.

Kasai's voice is sonorous and growling in my ear, I feel the jaguar's purr, the emerald eyes haunt me still. The monkey demons, all of their lewd gestures, and salacious comments run races around my mind. I pick up the pace. I'm going too fast and hit my shoulder into an oak.

I fall down on my back into the snow. Wincing, I grab my shoulder and squeak. It stings with such ferocity I'm sick to my stomach. I turn over and vomit.

"Hey, little mouse. You okay?" asks a familiar voice from up in the trees. It's the tiger demon. Another perverted cat seeking to ruin me. He can't though. I'm already ruined.

"No!" I shout. With the ocean cascading down my face I run deeper into the forest.

"Hey! Little mouse! You're going to hurt yourself."

The tiger demon is chasing after me.

"Leave me alone!" I scream.

There's nothing I have that is of any worth to this man anyway. I've been violated and used. I am a shell, a ghost, unreal. I'm too distracted by the tiger demon to notice the red rivers running down my thighs. I take a moment to pause but for some reason I don't feel protective and continue to run at breakneck speed.

"You're bleeding. Hey! Stop!"

Torao is quite fast and stays right behind me. Too close for comfort.

"Why do you care?" I yell over my shoulder.

"Pretty boy must be worried sick about you. Get back here!" shouts Torao.

"He doesn't love me!"

The words leave blisters in my gums. It's a sore on the roof of my mouth.

"That's the most ridiculous thing I have ever heard!"

The wildcat laughs before he pounces. He's on top of me, looking into my crimson eyes with his piercing sapphires.

"Hey! Get off of me!" I thrash but Torao is muscular and very heavy.

I continue to flail anyway. In the abyss of silky pink I feel more blood escape me. Torao turns me over and pins my wrists with his massive hand. His knees are pressing into my thighs. The tiger demon is going to violate me and make me watch him do it. I glare at him.

"Do it!" I shout.

"Do what? I'm trying to help you," he says.

"Doesn't feel like you're helping me," I spit at him.

Torao chuckles and the wildcat trill floats in the air. He takes his free hand and puts it in my kimono. To my surprise it doesn't roam, it rests where the stars are below my navel. His eyes brighten and his cheekbone pops out from his smirk.

"You're pregnant," he purrs.

For some reason this makes me feel horrible and I start to cry. The tiger demon looks at me confused.

"Hey, calm down. You and pretty boy are too in love to be acting like this," Toroa is genuine in his consideration.

"How would you know?"

I give up fighting him and lay down. He lowers himself on top of me so we are eye to eye and nose to nose.

"Because I see everything, little mouse. I've never seen two people in love the way you and him are."

It's the last thing I hear. He kisses me hard on the mouth and I succumb to the dark.

There are a thousand red and black eyes staring at me. Demons of all sorts. They have goat heads, horns, and fangs. Their feet are cracked hooves and their hands have sharp talons. I am standing on a platform. The first row of demons bow and then the next. So many of them kneel and bow to me. Why?

The sea of demons parts and he walks the dusty path towards me. Kasai in his red cloak. Enormous muscles ripple under his tan skin. It reminds me of black tea with a dash of milk. It's appalling but I keep staring at him. The vulture skull he wears covers his face but exposes his mouth and chin. The serpent tongue slides out of his lips and tastes the air.

"Come with me, Katan." Kasai takes my hand and I do not fight him. The demons bow to me.

"Queen Katan! Queen Katan!"

The booming voices echo against the walls of The Underworld dripping black tar and pus. There are basins of blood lining the edges. Upon further inspection I see body parts float to the top and hear a groaning sound from within the crimson soup. My hand grips Kasai's and I follow him without protest. I wish to let go but I can't.

"Where are you taking me?" I ask.

Kasai stops walking. He turns and his shadow consumes me. He is taller than Riku. Much taller. Kneeling down he lifts the vulture skull to look into my eyes that are his eyes. With his tan hands he holds my face and kisses me.

"I'm taking you home," he says.

His grip on my wrist is tight but not as tight as Riku's. The halls are dim and lit with ancient lanterns. Eyes wet with green and yellow mucus open as we pass. I feel something wet drip down into my kimono. With my free hand I touch it to see that it's blood. I look up and see the ceiling raining scarlet water. Bats and moths fly overhead. Their fluttering is overwhelming and makes my skin itch.

Kasai opens the door to a castle and guides me inside. It's lavish but morbid. There are chimeras trapped in cages. They yowl and screech. The wooden floor is decorated with beautiful rugs in dark red, black, and gold. There is a large pool of sheer red ink. I don't dare ask what that's for. His boots are loud with his weighted steps. We get to a room with a red and black door. I don't want to go in here.

"Please, let me go," I whisper.

Kasai's huge body heaves with laughter. It rumbles in his throat and chest. I hear the walls laugh with him and the infected eyes move with glee. They are amused by my plea. Kasai shoves me in the room and pushes me against the wall.

"Never," he hisses as the serpent tongue moves over my mouth and in my ear.

"Stop."

I try to push him away but he is massive and holds me with his meaty arm.

To my horror Kasai begins panting in my ear and touching where the stars are. The worst part is when I close my eyes he feels just like Riku.

I wake up and turn to my side to vomit. Brother Minoru holds my hair and Lady Kiyori offers me water after I empty my stomach.

"Aiya, are you alright?" asks Brother Minoru. His eyes have dark circles under them but he gives me a smile.

"Yeah," I lie.

"Are you having bad dreams again?" asks Lady Kiyori.

"No," I lie again. She is unsatisfied with my answer but nods.

"Brother Minoru and I are going to get you some medicine and food. We'll be right back," says Lady Kiyori.

"Okay," I rasp.

They leave and I lay back down. I've never wanted to kill myself but I think about it until they come back.

CHAPTER TWENTY

Tar Black Heart

"My beautiful wife, Queen Katan."

"I am not your queen."

"Then why do my people bow to you? Why would they treat you with such respect if you were not mine?" Kasai keeps reaching for me but I pace the room and dodge his advances.

"I don't know. This isn't real. You're dead," I spit.

"I live on inside you, Aiya. Your eyes, your claws, your eternal youth, I gave you those." I don't know what to say and I move past him again. "Why do you fight your love for me?" he asks.

"I don't love you."

"We'll see about that."

The fire demon lunges at me and is successful. I'm in his arms and his tongue is in my mouth.

Riku has been gone for two days. I have a feeling he's not coming back. Chiyo says I shouldn't worry but what does she know? Hajime is perfect. I chide myself on my hateful thoughts but they keep pouring in like a blizzard.

The dreams about Kasai have rotted my core. I feel vulgar. There is venom on my lips and rage in my soul. The baby inside me doesn't even make me happy anymore. Riku abandoned us like I knew he would. I wanted him and waited for him. This is how he leaves me. In pieces, alone, with his child.

I'm looking at my kimonos and eye the red one. Taking it in my arms I see the glint of something shiny. It's the knife Hajime made me. I don't carry it with me all the time anymore but I cherish it. It's excellently crafted. A work of art. The blade is perfect. Touching it softly my palm lingers and I cut myself. It stings but feels good. I put it to my wrist, not too hard, just enough to get a small river. Something breaks me and the knife is inside me. I'm stabbing the stars, cutting them up, they are exploding where the creation lies.

"Aiya!" Brother Minoru knocks the blade out of my hand. "Aiya! What are you doing?" He rips off his sleeve and puts pressure to the wound. I want to say something but I can't. He keeps calling my name but I disappear inside myself.

"I love you."

"I love you," the words are toxic and salty on my tongue.

"That's my girl," Kasai coos at me as he strokes my long hair.

I'm sitting on his lap. The throne we share is gold and embellished with jewels of every color. The cushion is lustrous and purple. The vulture skull is propped up so we can look at each other.

"Who am I?" I ask.

"Your name is Katan."

"Who gave me that name?"

"I did," he says.

"Why?"

"Stop asking so many questions and just be with me." He is agitated. I don't want to fight.

"Okay," I whisper. He kisses me and I embrace him.

"I've always been here for you, Katan. You know that, don't you?"

"Yes."

"Not like Riku who left you pregnant and alone. I'll take good care of you," he says and kisses the top of my head.

I wake up thrashing and screaming.

"Aiya! Please, stop. You're opening your wound," says Brother Minoru.

On my flat stomach is a large bandage seeping red ink out the bottom. It pools beside me and leaves a puddle on the white silk sheets. I'm not in my bed. This is Lady Kiyori's house.

"Let me go!" I scream. Lady Kiyori comes in with a bowl of rice and vegetables.

"Please eat something. You haven't eaten in two days," her voice is kind but it makes me angry.

"No!"

I go to knock the bowl out of her hand but realize I am restrained. There are silky ropes holding me down. I think of Kasai panting in my ear and my voice saying I love him. The tears run wild from my eyes that belong to him. I'm surprised they aren't red, too.

"Why are you doing this to me?" I whine.

"We are trying to help you," says Brother Minoru.

"Help me? That's a cruel joke!" I thrash again and more scarlet waves break the sand.

"Aiya, please stop," says the priestess. Lady Kiyori is always telling me what to do.

"Shut up! Just leave me alone." I can't control myself any longer. I'm pulling and flailing. I scream and no matter what the river runs through me and I can't see.

"Aiya—" says Brother Minoru who is changing my bandage.

It keeps opening. A deep gash crosses over the stars. The constellation has a black hole in it.

"Let me go. Stop! You're hurting me!" I scream.

Brother Minoru applies pressure to my injury and holds me down. I can't help but feel sorry for myself and cry more. It's brutal but I want my baby to die.

I can't have something that reminds me of him. At first I think it's a dream but it's really him. Riku is back. His face is long and sad. His deep set eyes watch me with a longing I haven't seen. There's a storm building inside him but I don't care. I want to die.

"You broke your promise." I narrow my eyes at him.

"What?" he asks.

"You said you would never leave me. You've been gone for three days. Look at me, Riku! Look at what they're doing to me!"

I pull at my restraints and feel the blood pour out of my cut. It aches but I like it. The stirring inside me is faint. The stars are going out one by one. Brother Minoru tries to stop me again.

"Please, Aiya. I am only trying to help you," he says but I spit in his face. I don't want him touching me. I don't want any more men touching me.

"I didn't leave you. I went to get you help. Please, Aiya. Please, come back to me."

My lover looks at me with his enchanting amber eyes. I always give in. They allow him everything.

"Your sad puppy dog eyes make me sick. Just get away from me!" I scream. Riku has large tears rolling down his cheek but I don't stop. I keep shredding him apart.

"Aiya..." Riku's voice is hardly above a whisper.

"I don't want this thing inside me and I don't want you!"

I take the ring off with my teeth and spit it at him. Riku darts out the door and Brother Minoru follows. I pull at the silky rope but can't free myself. Laying down I hear Kasai grunting and whispering in my ear. I toss and turn trying to get away but I can't.

A beautiful woman with wavy white hair and gold eyes kneels down next to me. I am mesmerized by her. She has an angelic face with well sculpted cheekbones. This must be Riku's sister. She is a mystifying ghost in a white kimono. Her hand is cool on my face. She touches the bandage without changing her expression.

"Who are you?" I ask.

"My name is Yama. I'm here to help you," she says. Her voice reminds me of a teacher's. It's pretty but she speaks like a scholar.

"No one can help me!" I shout at her.

She touches my feverish face with her icy hands that resemble Riku's and there is nothing.

***

Kasai has me locked up in this room in his castle. It's extravagant but I hate it. The bed is lustrous and covered in black sheets and red blankets. I don't touch it. The window is where I stand most of the time. My kimono is short and my shoes have high heels on them. Kasai's underlings do my hair and nails. They don't speak. The cloaks have large hoods that hide their faces. I do not know what they look like.

There are monsters in the sandy hills. They appear to be lacking intellect and wander with no purpose. They moan in pain and make creaking noises as they trudge through the desert of The Underworld. It rains scarlet drops and an orange haze appears as the black sun goes down. Time isn't real down here. It's all an illusion.

A chimera with wings flies by the window and yowls. It's hideous but intriguing. I'm not sure but I think the demons create the chimeras for entertainment. I see them in cages being transported to an arena where they fight to the death. Shiny scarlet liquid splatters across the wall in big globs. The bones break with ease, these creatures aren't made with integrity.

Everything smells like decay and poison. It's acidic and tickles my nose. The steam and red mist cause a humid environment. The walls sweat, the ceiling bleeds, pus filled blisters pop and drip out of blinking eyes. My arms are bruised purple and green from Kasai's constant hold on me. I massage my wrists and grimace.

It looks translucent. I think it is a mirage in the red sand and endless brick maze. Is it a ghost or is it my lover? I see him. He's with Hajime. I put my hand to the glass and call for him. I hit it but it won't break. The door is locked. I'm throwing everything in the room about. I pick up a chair and hit the window. It doesn't even leave a crack.

"Riku!" I call his name.

He can't hear me. They are unaware of the castle and don't notice it.

"Riku! I love you! Please, come back!" I call for him.

I plead for him to stay but he is gone. The stormy clouds drown them out in red ink painting the dunes.

"It's time to let him go, Katan. Time to let them all go."

Kasai is in the room with me.

"Never! I'll never let you take him away from me!"

"He's already gone," he says.

Kasai kisses me and I fall onto the black silk bed.

***

"Why are you doing this to me?"

I'm sitting with Kasai in his bloody hot spring. It disturbs me but I have no choice. He has his arm around me. I'm frozen inside myself.

"Because you're letting me," he coos and picks up a lock of hair. He twirls it around his finger.

"I would never do that," I say.

"You did though. You were the one who let the darkness in."

I see body parts floating in this demented pool of crimson water. Holding back my scream I remain calm on the surface.

"What do you mean?"

"Your doubts, your jealousy, they were my way into your heart. I saw that you didn't trust Riku completely anymore. I was there when you got that twinge of envy towards your best friend. It was delicious. Like cinnamon and blood oranges," he licks his lips at the word "blood."

"No," I say under my breath.

"Every time you have hatred towards someone, I am there. When you are reckless I am your muse. The days where you are chaotic and mean, it is me whispering to you. Hiding your pregnancy and being selfish, those are my favorite. Your love for Riku left your heart tattered and gave me plenty of opportunities. You can defy me but you are mine. I am a part of you."

"Stop!" I shout.

"No, Katan. You let me in. You wanted this," he laughs and a fire barrier appears around us. Not that I could escape anyway.

"I don't want this. You're forcing me," I hiss.

I look up at him and see my eyes staring back at me. His cheekbones are chiseled. He has a mole on his left cheek but it's attractive. How can someone be so handsome and hideous at the same time?

"The darkness tells me otherwise. It's been growing inside you. Do you see my face when you're with him? Do you feel my grasp on you as you lose yourself to the demonic rage?" he says and his fit of laughter kicks up the flames.

His huge chest moves with his amused howling. I want to slap him but I can't move.

"I'll never love you. This is a sick fantasy."

I break from his iron grip and get out of the morbid hot spring. Kasai looks shocked. I think he is going to hit me but he relaxes back into the bloody water.

"It's not a fantasy, Katan. You're already mine."

"That's not true," I say.

"Prove it," his tongue slithers towards me and enters my mouth.

I bite it and it recoils like a snake. Kasai really looks like he's going to hit me. I want him to. He stares at my nude body as I leave his room and run down the hall crying.

I am more than ponds, lakes, and rivers. My tears could fill the ocean. There is a crater in my heart filling up with soot and black tar. I don't want to be his but I feel his hold on me. It calls me back to him.

I run to the room with a red door and black symbol. Throwing myself on the bed I sob until I am a desert. Looking out the window I watch a chimera fly by. A ruby sandstorm is taking place and it knocks the creature around. It roars and uses its stretchy wings resembling a bat's to glide on the wind.

If I kill myself I will be trapped down here forever. I consider it but fight the urge. Even in this horrible place I have a glint of hope. There is a voice in my head I can't place but it comforts me, "Have faith, Aiya. Faith is what keeps us alive."

***

I'm wandering down a red brick hall. The floor is made of crimson dust. Lanterns are lit but it's still dark. Where am I going? It seems like every waking hour Kasai has his hands all over me. I am relieved to have a moment to myself. The moment is over before it has begun and I am in a terrible place.

It's a dungeon with dripping walls and eyes watching me as I pass by. Tiny voices say "hi, hi" in raspy tones. I think they are coming from the eyes but I'm not sure. It's disgusting the noise they make as they blink. I walk faster to get away from them.

There are several bodies chained to the walls. They are unconscious. I walk around the room to further inspect them. Are they dead? Is Kasai trying to trick me? The first one I approach is a woman with red trousers and long dark hair tied in a paper ribbon. Who is she? The man next to her has short hair and wears a blue robe. His necklace is wrapped around his wrist.

Across the dingy dungeon are more bodies. There is a man with a square jaw and other handsome features. These people are familiar to me but I can't place them. My name is Katan. Who are they? Sitting to his left is a woman my age. She has a widow's peak and shoulder length hair. It's straight and dark. Her face is pretty: delicate nose and berry lips.

In the darker part of the room are two more bodies. I gasp at the man. Kneeling down I see he has a gorgeous face. His hair is snowy white. I long to run my fingers through it. What's gotten into me? Holding up his chin to see him better I feel a twinge in my heart. Who is this man? I need to know.

I spend hours touching the man's face and hair trying to remember. There is something about him, something special. I know he is important to me. The armor he wears is heavy. It appears to be expensive. His hands are twice the size of mine. I have fair skin but he is fairer than I. A beautiful ghost.

Unable to figure out his name I turn to the woman sitting next to him. She is fascinating. An attractive woman with sparkly silver hair. She has fox ears on top of her head. Her hands are elegant, thin fingers and slender palms. Short but thick eyelashes accent her face. They remind me of bird wings. It's barely a glimpse but I see something. An image of this woman and me laughing in the forest.

It fades but I call it back. I wait for a long time before anything happens. Her and I are walking. I tell her I am searching for someone but I don't know their name. She looks at me with wide chestnut eyes.

The voices of Kasai's castle cackle and laugh at me. They know I can't figure out the cruel joke he's playing on me. I begin to sob. There is a shift in the energy and I feel a sting in my spine.

"Aiya? Can you hear me?" says a clear and pleasant male voice.

I look around but no one is talking to me. Is it the eyes? The voice speaks again, "Aiya, it's me. Hajime."

A memory comes back to me. He gave me a present on my birthday, a knife. I turn around and look at the man with a square jaw. That voice belongs to this man. He is Hajime.

"Aiya, remember him. I know you can remember him," he says. Where is he? The eyes weep yellow pus and close in succession. I think the voice is having a negative effect on them.

"Remember who?" I ask the room.

"Remember the first time you heard his name. I know you can do this, Aiya. I believe in you."

The voice is calm and comforting. I scoot closer to the man with white hair and the fox woman.

"His name is Riku. The disgraced wolf prince," the fox woman's voice is high and shimmery.

Riku! That's his name. The man I love, the reason why I sing, my winter, my everything. I see it now. A flash of memories overwhelm me but I light up as they fly through my mind like a thousand cranes. My racing thoughts pause on an image. It's a baby boy. He looks just like Riku. The same cheekbones and chin. They have gold eyes and snowy hair. Freckles kiss his nose. This is our baby.

"Do you remember him, Aiya?" asks Hajime's voice.

It echoes against the dungeon walls. The ceiling is caving in. Infected eyes blink rapidly and squirm in their sockets. I hold the shoulders of the man with white hair as the room collapses around me. Bats dart past me. Pieces of the crumbling dungeon fall and squish the unlucky ones.

"His name is Riku."

CHAPTER TWENTY ONE

Your Name

It seems too good to be true but I wake up with Riku wrapped around my waist. He has his ear pressed up to the stars. My wound, the blackhole, is gone. It has been replaced by another constellation, Scorpio. I touch the skin below my navel with a ginger hand. It's faint but there is a light pulse. Tears of joy spill out and I feel so glad our baby is okay. That is until I realize what I did. I tried to cut him out. Continuing to cry until there is no water left in the sorrowful ocean I relax.

Riku's face is covered in blood. He smells metallic and like he's been set on fire. The Underworld, him and Hajime went down there for me. They would do anything for me. I hope no one is mad at me for my horrendous behavior. I recall every terrible thing I did and the ocean refills and pours out. Will I be forgiven? I touch Riku's hair and rub his shoulder. He's in a deep sleep. It must have been a harrowing experience for him and Hajime down there. I don't want to wake him up but I miss him and when I miss him I sing.

The wolf was once lonely
But never again
He is my one
He is my only
We were once two
Now we're a family

***

"Aiya," he perks up right away. Riku saying my name is frosty and beautiful.

"Hi."

He kisses me and I hold him. It makes my heart flutter holding him in my arms. I thought I'd never see him again. How could I have forgotten his name for even a moment?

"I thought I lost you," whispers Riku.

He picks up a portion of my hair and wraps it around his wrist. I hold his flawless face and rub his nose with mine. He is covered in The Underworld's blood but I don't care. He's smiling and looking at me like there is nothing and no one else. It hits me in my soul. Our baby, I almost destroyed our family.

"Riku, I did such an ugly thing. I am so sorry. Can you ever forgive me?" I sob with such incredible force it causes me to shiver.

Riku rubs my back and reassures me as I knew he would but I feel guilty. He risked his life for me. I owe Hajime my thanks as well. It was his voice that guided me out of my prison.

"Don't say sorry. I know your heart. That wasn't you," he says.

"I love our baby. You have to know how much I want them," I sob. Riku looks at me with sympathetic eyes. He has no words but kisses me at least a hundred times.

"I know you do. You loved them first."

Riku speaks with such eloquence when I am at a loss for words. I pull him into my arms and we lay tangled up in each other's web until Lady Kiyori knocks at the door.

"Come in," I call.

She's brought us soup and rice. I'm not hungry but I know I should eat. Lady Kiyori is a wonderful person. She reminds me of my mother. "Thank you," I say. My voice is quiet.

"You're welcome. How are you feeling, Aiya?" she asks.

"Kind of dizzy."

"You'll feel better after you eat. What about you, Riku?"

She gives him a mischievous glance. I think she has become quite fond of him. He trusted her to help me when we were lost. He must be fond of her, too.

"I'm good. I'm happy to have my family back," he says.

This is the first time Riku has referred to me or the baby as his family. I am touched. A grin stretches across my face. I see Lady Kiyori is wearing a smile as well.

"Good. I'm glad. Oh, I forgot to give you this," she says.

Lady Kiyori hands him my buttercup and spider lily kimono. The one that I was wearing when I ran off. It was soaked in blood but now it looks new.

"I thought this was ruined. Thank you," he says with gratitude. I know it holds great importance to him.

"I have a little magic of my own," says Lady Kiyori.

She winks at Riku. He seems surprised but smiles. This makes me giggle and I lift myself up so I can kiss his neck.

"You two probably want to be alone. I'll check on you tomorrow."

Lady Kiyori makes a swift exit. I turn to Riku and he pulls me towards him. I listen to his heart. It's even and resounding. This must be what happiness sounds like. He rests his hand on the stars of my navel. I feel the pulse in the depths of the night sky and its aliveness lights a fire inside. I get excited and sit up.

"Riku, do you want to know what our baby looks like?" I ask.

I put my hand over his and we lock eyes for a moment. He thinks about it with consideration as I knew he would. His son will be in his image and have stars on his face.

"No. I want it to be a surprise," he says.

Riku is relaxed and content. This is the happiest I think I've ever seen him. I have seen him have happy moments but Riku is different now. He's here with me without the distance between us.

"I love you," I say.

"I love you, too."

He pulls me down to lay with him. There was always something keeping him from me but not anymore.

Riku was once an island I could never reach. A storm I would chase but never fully experience. The lone wolf who didn't know how loved he was. In his arms I am everything. I hold my starry night and smile.

"Riku?"

"Yes?" His voice is softer than usual. It's nice.

"It was Hanako who told me your name. That's how I knew it."

My fox friend. A cherished person. A girl who has been through awful things but never stops smiling. Hanako is a hero in her own way. She should be here in a few weeks. The cherry blossoms haven't bloomed yet. There is still snow on the ground but I look forward to seeing her.

"I am forever indebted to Hanako," he sighs.

"I can't wait to tell her that I'm pregnant," I say and close my eyes to better see beneath the constellation.

"She's going to be really happy."

Riku is at ease. I like seeing him like this. Even though there is blood on his face he is gorgeous. The most stunning person I have ever seen. To me he looks like a god.

"We're all going to be really happy."

I sit up to kiss him. Lifting up his bangs I study his beautiful gold eyes. I missed them. They hold everything: sympathy, love, hope, sorrow, desire, and ice. Riku doesn't retreat inside himself or travel to the moon. He is no longer in one hundred places at once.

We fall asleep. I dream of our reunion in the summer. It makes my heart swell. My dreams show me our baby. I see Riku holding our son this fall with rainbow leaves drifting all around them. We are a family. Riku has been my savior, a distant dream, my lover, my army. Soon I will be his wife. When I wake I reach for him. I look up to see he is watching over me with those puppy dog eyes.

***

Riku has stepped out to get me medicine. He didn't want to go but it's necessary. Feeling protective and worried he asked Chiyo to sit with me while he's out. I feel ashamed of my jealousy towards her. Hajime risked his life to save me. He is my friend. I know he loved me but they are meant to be. I can see that now.

"How are you feeling, Aiya? I was so worried about you," says my sweet best friend.

She is braiding my hair. Her small hands and nimble fingers are familiar. Chiyo smiles at me like I am wonderful and it floods my blood with sugar.

"Much better. Thank you for visiting me. I apologize for my

strange behavior," I start but Chiyo cuts me off.

"Don't worry about it. You never have to worry about that stuff with me. I know who you really are. I know you inside and out," the bells in her voice ring. I put my arms around her.

"You are too kind," I whisper.

"I love you," she says through her smile.

"I love you, Chiyo."

I pull away and brush a lock of black ink from her face. "I know you love Hajime," I announce. She holds her arm and squeezes it with discomfort.

"Yes. He proposed to me last month. I said 'yes.' I hope you're not mad at me," she says in a grave tone not meant for her musical voice.

"Of course not. You two are perfect for each other. I wish you both nothing but happiness." I am sincere. No hint of glowing envy or irritation.

"Thank you, Aiya." Chiyo continues to play with my hair until Riku arrives.

"Hey," he greets us. On his handsome face he wears a smile fit for the gods. It's quite charming on him.

"Hi," I say. Riku hands me an apple and a clear vial with pink liquid in it.

"What's this?" I ask.

"The man at the apothecary said it would help with your nausea and speed up your recovery," he says. Chiyo and I look at each other and giggle.

"What?" he asks. He is tilting his head the way a dog would again. Chiyo hides her smile behind her hand but mine escapes me.

"Nothing. You just seem different," I say.

"I am different." He is. Chiyo gets up and heads for the door.

"I'm going to go home but I'll bring you guys dinner tonight, okay?" she says.

"You don't have to do that," I say but she protests.

"I want to! Bye. See you later!"

"Bye! Thank you!" I say as loud as I can. My voice is still weak.

"Bye Chiyo," says Riku. He gets into bed with me and pulls me to his chest. I lean on him as I drink the medicine and nibble on the apple.

"I missed you. Did you miss me?" he asks.

"I always miss you."

"You don't have to miss me anymore. I'm right here."

He rests his hand on the airy pulse and puts his strong arm around me but not too tight.

***

Riku and I are fire and ice. He is my forever winter. The evergreen forest I explore. Every day I venture deeper into the place where he would disappear. Riku doesn't hide from me anymore. If I sense I am losing him he is easy to call back. All I have to do is sing. It is his anchor. I am the siren luring him out to sea. He is my one, my only, my everything.

At night I look up at the moon. *Why did the wolf god choose me? What makes me special?* I remain eternally thankful. My life held little importance to me until my transformation. I had to save an entire village to care about myself. The fire demon may have mutilated parts of my soul but I am free now. It will take time to heal the broken pieces and soothe the burnt edges but I can handle it.

There is a bond between Riku and I and it's unbreakable. An undeniable connection. I was worried he didn't feel it but he does. I know he does. He went into The Underworld for me. Riku is my army. I do not fear anything if he is by my side. He thinks Hajime saved me but it was his name that made the walls of The Underworld collapse.

Riku has been my wildest dream. Nothing could have prepared me for such a blizzard. The embers of his heart belong to me. I melt away the ice and it turns to rain. He is the moon and I am the stars. We collide and create something shining brighter than silver or jewels. Riku is holding me. I catch him watching me as I admire the sunrise.

"What are you thinking about?" he asks.

A monk and a priestess raised me. My best friend is strawberry sunshine and ocean waves. A man I rejected cares for me enough to assist my lover in The Underworld. The fox princess taught me we can still be joyful even though we've been hurt.

Pain teaches us things that nothing else can. I thought I was no one but I am the girl who fell in love with a wolf. The one who has been everything, seen everywhere. Our child's feathery pulse gives me goosebumps.

"How my life has changed. I thought I had no family but my family keeps growing. I'm lucky," I say. My voice is small but I am content.

"We both are," says Riku.

He prefers sunsets to sunrises but he wakes up to watch them with me. Our favorite season is winter. His favorite color is green. He likes baby blue bells. I think they remind him of the northern mountains.

Riku thought he wasn't worthy of love but that's not true. We both have a past but that doesn't mean we are bad. Everyone has a story. Love is accepting the tattered pages. It requires patience. He is frosty pine needles. My kiss dissolves the snow. I think he accepts my love now because he finally accepts himself.

THE END

Other Fine Books by Tawnya Torres

A Silent Discovery
Heart of the Machine
The Soul Keeper's Assistant
To Know Your Name
Bloodlust

9 781958 557556